MOON KISSED

THE MARKED WOLF TRILOGY

JEN L. GREY

Copyright © 2021 by Jen L. Grey

All rights reserved.

No part of this book may be reproduced in any form or by any electronic or mechanical means, including information storage and retrieval systems, without written permission from the author, except for the use of brief quotations in a book review.

CHAPTER ONE

About Four Years Ago

Emma

The cool April breeze blew, rustling the leaves and low branches hiding us, but it couldn't calm the heat running through my body. Aidan sat next to me, and I stared into his gorgeous golden eyes that always held a faint glow—evidence of his strong wolf inside.

"I hate that I can't come to your birthday party." He ran his fingertips across my cheeks, and his piney scent filled my nose. "Turning fourteen is a big deal."

Fourteen years ago, my adoptive parents had found me here, and I'd been drawn to this spot ever since. Then, one fateful night, two years ago, his wolf had brought him to me. We'd been coming here at least three times a week around midnight ever since, and I was closer to him than anyone else. But it didn't matter. Our packs were not friendly due to a feud that went back so far that no one in my pack remembered the cause. And though it didn't matter, the pack would still frown upon him coming to the party.

"I hate it too." My blood always buzzed inside me, though it amplified around him. But, hell, it could have just been the butterflies flitting about inside my stomach. I'd always enjoyed his company, but these past few months, my feelings for him had been strengthening. "I'd do anything to have you there," I'd whispered, and his wolf hearing picked up each and every word.

"One day, they won't be able to tell us what to do." He cleared his throat and scooted closer to me. He tugged at his black shirt as his shoulder touched mine.

"Until then, we at least have these moments together." I always counted down to these moments when we'd sneak out of our homes to come here and spend a couple of hours together under the moon.

His gaze traveled to my lips.

I wanted to yell at him to kiss me, but I was also relieved he hadn't. I'd been practicing with my mirror since I'd never been kissed before. He was the only boy I'd ever held hands with. I wanted him to be my first everything.

"I know it's not until tomorrow, but I have something for you." He leaned away from me and reached into his jeans pocket. He pulled out a leather cord with a wooden heart painted red dangling from it. "It's not much, but I wanted you to have a piece of me there with you."

My fingers brushed the warm, smooth surface before I took the entire heart in my hand. "I love it."

He nibbled his bottom lip. "I made it for you. No matter where you are, my heart is yours." He stiffened as the words left his mouth, and he watched me out of the corner of his eye.

My heart beat a little faster. "You have mine, too."

He blew out a breath and took my hand in his. "Really?"

"Yes." The weight of the moment hit me hard. He felt the same way I did about him.

"May I ..." He nibbled his lip again as his eyes landed on mine. "Uh ... kiss you?"

Unable to form words, I nodded.

A grin spread across his face as he slowly leaned in. He paused for a second as he stared into my eyes. "I love you, Emma."

Before I could respond, his lips touched mine.

I closed my eyes and followed his lead. He deepened the kiss, and my heart hammered so hard it rang in my ears.

This was better than anything I could've ever imagined. He tasted of minty toothpaste, and it was now my favorite taste in the world.

Our lips parted, and he gave me a huge smile. "Can I put the necklace on you?"

"Huh?" It took a second for the words to make sense in my head. "Oh, yeah. Please." I handed the necklace back to him and turned around.

I moved my long blonde hair aside and waited for him to place the necklace over my head. When he didn't, I looked back.

His brows were furrowed, and confusion filled his eyes.

"Are you okay?" He'd been here with me a moment ago, but now he was miles away.

"Uh... yeah." He stood in a rush and brushed the grass off his jeans. "I've got to go. I'm sorry." He turned and walked away, leaving me behind.

Aidan

My eyes had to be playing tricks on me. Did the girl I love have the mark of my enemy?

The confusion in her eyes hurt, but I had to leave. I hid in the woods and turned around to see her gorgeous gray eyes locked on where I'd disappeared. Her body tensed as her hand clutched the heart I'd just given her.

There was no way she could be bad… or a monster. Even though my wolf howled deep within me, I knew what I had to do. I needed to stay away to protect her.

Emma

The party felt like it would never end. The entire pack was here, in the large open clubhouse at the center of the neighborhood, to celebrate my birthday. People were dancing like they didn't have a care in the world.

Even though we weren't sure when I was born, we celebrated my birthday on April eighteenth, the day my parents found me abandoned in the woods. Apparently, there had been a dead shifter in wolf form right beside me. They believed it was my father, but no one knew for certain.

My parents had been trying for a child for so long they hadn't hesitated to take me in. They'd seen it as a blessing, and it had seemed like fate since I was a wolf as well. The Rogers pack accepted me as if I were their blood. Even though none of them threatened me, I was ready to lose everything at any second. How could these people love me when my own parents hadn't wanted me?

Even if the wolf had been my father, it didn't change

how I felt—I needed to be the perfect daughter and wolf for my parents and the pack.

I sat at the table closest to the cake and watched as people laughed, smiled, danced, and talked to one another.

"Hey, Emma." Jacob sat next to me. He was the alpha's son and the guy all the girls in school and in our wolf pack wanted. "Why are you on the sidelines? It's your birthday. You should be out there with Libby and Grace, dancing."

Libby and Grace were my two best friends in the entire world, and I probably should have been dancing with them, but I just wanted to see Aidan. He'd left in such a weird way last night, and I was panicking. Maybe I was a horrible kisser and I'd ruined everything between us.

"Earth to Emma." Jacob touched my shoulder. His chocolate-brown eyes found mine through his shaggy hair.

"Yeah, sorry." I had to stop stressing. Mom had already called me out for acting off tonight, and now Jacob. "I guess it's surreal. I'll be a freshman next school year."

"Ah, so you're feeling old." He chuckled and winked at me. "Don't worry. Age looks good on you."

Oh, ew. I hadn't expected that. If I wasn't all caught up in Aidan, I'd probably be into Jacob, but he paled in comparison. No one else in the world was meant for me. "Uh... thanks?" I hadn't meant for it to come out as a question.

"I mean it." He grinned. "I've been trying to get you to notice me for a while, but you're always so distant.'

"You're in high school." Thankfully, that came out instead of the real reason I didn't want to be with him. The last thing I needed to do was upset him and his father.

"And, as you pointed out, you'll be there in just a few short months." He shrugged and scooted closer to me. "I'm only a year older."

He wasn't going to let this go.

"Hey, Emma." Grace had a shit-eating grin on her face as she hurried over. "Whatcha doing?" She waggled her eyebrows right in front of Jacob.

I wanted to die of embarrassment. I wished an earthquake would hit and the ground would swallow me whole.

Grace giggled and ran her fingers through her dark auburn curls, and then she pulled at her green dress that was almost the same shade as her eyes.

"Well, I'd hoped to ask her on a date, but you interrupted me." Jacob's eyes stayed on me, watching for my reaction.

"Oh my God," Grace squealed and jumped up and down. "Okay, I'll go over there, so don't mind me." She rushed over to Libby and whispered into her ear.

Great, this was getting out of hand. I didn't want to date Jacob, but what the hell could I do?

"So... what do you say?" His fingers tapped on the table.

"I'm too young to date." In my defense, my parents were overprotective, so it was a good excuse.

"Okay, I'll talk to your parents." Jacob leaned over, and his eyes landed on my necklace. "Oh, is that new?"

"Uh... no." I didn't know what else to say. If I'd told him yes, he would have wanted to know who'd given it to me. I touched the pendant, which already meant so much to me.

"It looks good on you." He smiled as he stood and said, "Happy birthday." He made a beeline to my parents.

I STEPPED out into the hallway and listened to my parents' deep breathing. It had taken forever, but finally, my parents were asleep. I hurried to my bedroom window and quietly slid it open.

Luckily, we lived in a ranch-style home. I climbed out of the window and glanced around to make sure none of our neighbors were out. All the houses backed up to the woods, and I raced into the trees, toward the territory line. I was so eager to see Aidan after our kiss last night. Maybe we could do a repeat.

I reached the small clearing and paused. Aidan was always here before me, but not this time. It was odd. This had never happened before. I sat down on my side of the territory line like I always did. We tried not to tempt fate too much by breaking the boundaries dictated centuries ago.

After a few minutes of waiting, I lay back on the grass and watched the moon. The breeze blew, and before I realized it, I'd fallen fast asleep.

Aidan

It took every ounce of strength I had not to run to her. She was waiting for me, her hand clutching the pendant I'd given her, and concern was etched on her forehead.

Even though we couldn't be together, it was up to me to keep her safe. I'd expected her to give up waiting and leave after an hour or so, but it was getting close to dawn. She must feel the same damn pull as I did.

Dad had almost caught me sneaking out tonight, reaffirming what I already knew: I couldn't let my dad and brother find out about her.

When she lay down and her eyes drifted closed, my

heart beat harder. I had to stay hidden, but how the hell was that possible when all I wanted was to hold her in my arms?

Emma

"Emma, are you okay?" Jacob's voice stirred me from my sleep.

My eyes fluttered open, and I slowly sat up. When I realized where I was, my heart began to race. He never came last night, and I'd stupidly fallen asleep, waiting for him.

"Your parents are worried sick." Jacob squatted beside me. "Did something happen?"

Tears burned my eyes. Aidan had never stood me up before. The one time he'd thought he wouldn't make it, he'd left me a message. He'd still beat me here, and I'd thought he had been sweet and considerate.

Jacob spoke loudly once more. "Emma."

"No, I needed to get out." I had no clue what I was saying. My body felt numb, and my heart hurt. "I couldn't sleep and needed fresh air."

"You're right on the border. You know we don't get along with that pack." Jacob took my hands in his and winced. "You're freezing. Come on." He helped me stand and tugged on my arm to lead me away.

I didn't want to leave. I needed to see Aidan.

"Emma, come on," Jacob said.

There was no point in resisting. I had to go, especially since Jacob was here. Even if Aidan showed up now, he wouldn't appear.

It made no sense. Something must have happened. Was

he hurt? There was no damn way I could find out. If I walked the territory line and demanded to see, it wouldn't go well.

I hadn't even realized I was walking until we broke through the tree line.

"Thank God." Mom ran out of the house and straight toward me. "Where have you been?"

"I needed fresh air last night." The words I'd told Jacob only minutes ago fell from my lips. "I fell asleep."

"Josh," Mom yelled, "she's here."

Dad rushed out the door and wrapped me in his arms. "Are you okay?"

"Yeah." I pulled out of his grasp, needing space and time alone. "I'm going inside to take a shower." I hurried into the house without bothering to look at their expressions.

"She was at the territory line." Jacob's voice was low, but I could still hear him.

"What for?" Mom asked.

Jacob sighed. "She didn't say."

"Was it the same spot as where we found her?" Dad sounded so concerned.

"Yeah, it was." Jacob paused and lowered his voice further. "I'm worried about her."

"It'll be fine. Thanks for finding her." Pride entered Dad's voice as he said, "You'll make a good alpha someday."

Not wanting to hear anymore, I walked into the bathroom and stared in the mirror. My usually gray eyes were so dark they looked like charcoal, and my long blonde hair was limp and greasy. Hell, even the cleft in my chin seemed more prominent. After a few seconds, I looked away from the girl I didn't recognize and took a shower.

I'd gone to the territory line every night for the past month, but not once had he appeared. Every night, my heart had hoped he'd be there, and every night, it had broken all over again. He had disappeared without a trace, and I didn't know why. At first, I'd been afraid he was hurt or worse, but there'd been no ceremonies at the sacred place where we buried our dead. All packs in Mount Juliet, Tennessee buried theirs there.

So, I could only assume he was choosing not to come. My heart was shattered, and I wasn't sure I'd ever be happy again. The boy I loved had left me behind, and I'd never gotten to say the words back to him.

CHAPTER TWO

Present Day

I tapped my foot incessantly when we breezed through the gates of Crawford University. My blood buzzed, which wasn't unusual, but it hadn't been this bad in a while. The buzzing was only this powerful when I was close to... him.

Four years later, it hurt just as much as the damn night he'd never shown. I had thought turning fourteen would change things for me. Had I known it would have been for the worse, I would've kissed him longer and forced him to tell me why he'd been acting so strange before he left.

"Hey, are you okay?" Jacob reached over the center console and placed his hand on my thigh.

It didn't feel the same way as when... Oh, my God. I had to stop. Even though he still consumed my thoughts, it was worse than normal. What the hell was going on with me? It had to be because I was going away to college where I'd have no chance of seeing him.

At home, I'd slip back to the border every so often. Hell,

I'd been there last night, begging for him to show, which was stupid. If he had shown his face, I would have wanted nothing to do with him. I couldn't chance getting hurt like this again. Even when Libby and Grace had gotten their hearts broken over their first loves, they'd licked their wounds and gotten back out there. Not me. My heart was still in pieces, and I was afraid it would never be whole again.

"We're here at college, finally," Jacob said, bringing me back to the present.

I shook my head and blinked. "What was the question?"

His brown eyes filled with concern. He always worried about me in some way. "If you were okay?"

"Oh, yeah." I waved it off with my other hand. "Just nerves."

"I'll be right beside you." Jacob's words sounded like a promise.

A promise I wasn't sure I wanted. He'd been after me since my fourteenth birthday. After two years of him asking both me and my parents, I finally went on a date with him. He and my parents had pestered me about it every day until I'd eventually agreed. How could I keep turning down the very people who'd taken me in when I was unwanted by my own flesh and blood? He was handsome, kind, and considerate—everything you'd ever want in a man—but I was broken. I was afraid to let anyone else in like I had with Aidan.

Aidan.

Shit. Even thinking his name affected me. It was time to get my shit together.

We turned onto a side road that took us past the business building and toward the dorms. His dorm was right next to mine, so it made moving our stuff in more convenient.

"Did your dad alert the local pack that we're attending here?" Colleges were neutral territories, but if we went off campus to hang out, they needed to know we weren't trying to invade them. One main pack controlled the small suburb here, only a half-hour north of Atlanta.

"Yeah, they said they appreciated the heads up." Jacob winked. "So, we're good, and I can take my girl out any time I want."

He was so damn sweet and patient but relentless. If I even hinted that I wasn't happy, he'd go crying to his dad and my parents. We'd done some things together, but we hadn't gone all the way. I couldn't bring myself to, but he had been clear that a wolf had needs, so some things were expected.

Even when I pushed him off, he never looked at another girl. For some reason, he was all-in with me. Grace swore it had to do with me being one of the few girls who weren't fawning all over him. I was a challenge that any strong alpha would love. She might have a point, but I wasn't doing it to be a challenge. The simple truth was that I could never love him the way he wanted me to. My heart had been taken years ago, and I still hadn't gotten it back.

My large brick building appeared, and he pulled into a parking spot. Several other people were doing the same thing.

"Ready?" He turned toward me with a smile, his brown hair still shaggy and falling into his eyes.

I couldn't help but smile at his boyish charm. "Yeah."

He bent down and waved his hand toward the building. "Then let's get you set up."

He climbed out of his Ford F250 truck and hurried over

to my side. He opened the door for me and took my hand to help me down. He towered over my five-foot-ten height, which was saying something. I was taller than half of the human men.

"Thank you." I took a deep breath, making sure I concentrated on the moment.

"You're welcome." He leaned down and brushed his lips against mine.

It felt nice, but that was it. When he tried to deepen the kiss, I stepped back.

I watched as he headed to the bed of his truck and opened the tailgate. He was muscular and cut in all the right places. He'd gone to a local college my senior year of high school, and because of him, they'd won the championship. After finding out I was going to Crawford University, he applied and received a full scholarship.

In a way, I'd wanted to come here alone—a fresh start without any baggage—but that dream had gone out of the window when he'd decided to come here with me.

Once we'd unloaded all of my things, we headed up to the dorm. Two girls were standing in the front, smiling.

"Hi," said the girl who had dark brown hair cascading over her shoulders as her hazel eyes scanned Jacob from head to toe. "I'm Caroline, one of the RA's here."

"Nice to meet you." He smiled as he dropped one of the bags to the ground and wrapped an arm around my waist. "I'm Jacob, and this is my girlfriend, Emma."

"Oh." Her eyes dimmed for a moment, but soon her smile was back. "It's nice to meet you both. This is Jules, another RA here."

"Do you know which one is your room?" Jules flipped her auburn hair over her shoulders as she batted her brown eyes.

It probably should have bothered me, but it didn't. One thing about us wolf shifters was that we had genetics on our side, and Jacob was one of the best-looking shifters in our pack.

"Yeah, it's on the second floor." I stepped out of Jacob's arm so he could pick up the bag again. "It's nice to meet you two." I walked around them as Jules giggled and lowered her voice to tell Jacob, "I hope to see you around soon."

"You sure will." His voice sounded fake, but I was sure neither of them noticed. "I'll be here a lot with Emma." He turned and left them in silence.

I opened the door to my room, and the musky smell of another wolf shifter hit my nose.

My roommate was a wolf shifter too. For some reason, that surprised me.

Jacob's eyes met mine, and he nodded toward the hall.

"Is that my roommate?" the girl called from inside.

I paused for a moment and stepped inside the room. "Yes, it sure is."

It was obvious when my scent hit her. Her blue eyes darkened, and her shoulders sagged. She pursed her lips and pulled her royal blue hair into a makeshift ponytail. "You're a shifter."

Not sure what that was supposed to mean, I replied, "Look, if you aren't cool with me rooming with you, I'd bet we can get someone to switch." I didn't want to feel unwelcome in my own room.

"No, I'm relieved." She dropped her hands back to her sides, and her eyes bounced from me to Jacob.

"Okay, good." Her being a wolf from a different pack could be a good thing. I wouldn't have to hide my supernatural abilities from her.

She tilted her head and bit her bottom lip. "It's fucking

perfect. If we need to leave in the middle of the night, we won't have to come up with excuses for needing to be in our animal form."

I hadn't thought of needing a run. "True."

"Well, it's settled." Jacob glanced at me and snapped.

"Make yourself at home." The girl placed her weight to one side, causing her right hip to jut out as she waved her hands around. She was different from the girls back home. Unique. She wore dark makeup with several layers of eyeshadow, which made her eyes pop. She wasn't even trying to go for the natural look.

And unlike most women, she didn't have any interest in Jacob. We might get along fine after all. "Okay, then." I used our pack's mind link to connect to him. *She's different.*

Yeah, she kind of reminds me of you. She marches to the beat of her own drum. He shrugged as he walked past me and placed my stuff down on the vacant bed to the left.

The room wasn't huge, but we each had our own bed and desk. She'd picked the side with the window, and I couldn't blame her. If I'd gotten here first, I'd have chosen it as well.

"So, I'm Beth," the girl said as she held out her hand to me. "I'm from a pack in Alabama."

It was nice that she focused on me and not Jacob. That wasn't the normal response I got from most girls. "I'm Emma, and this is Jacob." I pointed to him.

"Her boyfriend." He moved closer to me.

She raised her eyebrows so high they disappeared under her short blue bangs. "Okay." The corners of her lips ticked upward as she nodded.

I placed the box that contained my sheets and pillows on the ground while Jacob rolled my two large suitcases over to me. My duffle bag and backpack stayed at the foot of my bed.

"Where do we start?" He clapped his hands, looking at the pile.

Yeah, no. This was something I wanted to do by myself as my first act of independence. "I appreciate your eagerness, but you have your own room to set up."

His face fell ever so slightly. "But..."

I had to word this carefully. I didn't want to hurt his feelings, or Lord knew I'd be getting a call from my mom. "Maybe when you're done with your room, you can swing back here, and we'll grab something to eat."

"Yeah." His eyes warmed. "We can definitely do that. I'll be back here after I drop off my stuff and check in with the coach."

"Sounds good."

"Okay, I'll see you soon." He kissed my lips briefly before walking out the door.

"That guy has it bad for you." Beth sat on her bed and shook her head. "It was hard to watch."

"We've been together for a while." I wasn't going to open up to someone within the first five minutes of meeting them.

"How long?" Beth asked as she watched me make my bed.

"A little over two years." It was two years after Aidan had broken my heart. Jacob had escorted me to my sixteenth birthday party, and my parents and his dad had gone on and on about how good we were together. He'd asked me out right in front of everyone. Sometimes, I couldn't help but wonder if it had been calculated. He knew I wanted to please my parents.

"It's obvious you aren't fated." She blew out a breath. "I hope to find my fated one day, don't you?"

"No, a chosen mate would be my preference." I couldn't risk what was left of my broken heart. Hell, I'd rather be alone, but my parents wanted grandbabies, and through Jacob, our pack needed to grow. If I'd been hurt that badly by my first love, I didn't want to imagine how excruciating it would be from a fated.

"Really?" Beth pursed her lips. "What happens if Lover Boy finds his?"

"First off, you make it sound like fated mates are a common occurrence. They aren't." I glanced over my shoulder at her. "So, it's not something I need to worry about."

"Well, okay then." She shrugged and lay back on her bed, her head pillowed on her arms as she watched me.

I decided to focus on setting up my room, not my nosey roommate.

A KNOCK on the door startled me out of my daydream.

"It's just your man." Beth snorted and glanced my way.

I'd just got situated a few minutes ago and had lain down to calm my racing thoughts. Of course he'd be back here already. Sometimes it felt like I couldn't breathe with him beside me. "Yeah, I was just thinking about something." I stood and headed over to the door to open it.

"Hey, you." He grinned as he entered the room, and his gaze landed on my roommate. He nodded at her. "Beth."

She nodded back, laughing. "Jacob."

He paused, and his brows furrowed. He wasn't used to someone making fun of him.

I glared at her. "Be nice."

"What?" She lifted both hands in the air. "I was being polite."

"Do you want to join us for dinner?" The question had left my mouth before I'd thought it all the way through. However, it'd be nice to have more than Jacob and his friends to keep me company.

Beth looked at Jacob. "You don't mind?"

"No, it's fine." He took my hand. "Some of the guys were heading down to the Student Center anyway, so the more, the merrier."

"Okay, sweet." Beth jumped to her feet and pulled her black shirt down over her jeans. Then, she slipped her sandals on. "Let's do this."

The three of us headed to the stairs and walked down to the student lobby.

I squeezed Jacob's hand. "Did you meet your roommate?"

"Sure did." He walked past Caroline and Jules without looking in their direction. "His name is Prescott Jones, and he transferred here like me to be on the football team."

"Prescott?" Beth bumped her shoulder into mine. "Must be old money."

"Actually, he is." Jacob pointed at her with his free hand. "You hit the mark. His grandfather was an oil investor."

"Sounds about right," she muttered.

I couldn't keep from grinning. Her bluntness was refreshing to be around.

We walked past the business center, and everyone appeared to be out and buzzing around. People were still lined up to learn more about fraternities and sororities. In general, wolf shifters didn't join things like that because growing too close to humans risked them learning about us, which was against supernatural law. That was one reason why I wasn't too upset about my wolf shifter roommate.

"What did your football coach say?" This past summer, he'd left for a couple of weeks to practice with the team. Surprise, surprise, he was the quarterback. Those two weeks had been way too short. I actually got to breathe for once. Sometimes it felt like I was trapped, but I wasn't sure what I needed to change to feel free. I still hoped that college would be my salvation.

"Nothing, just glad that I'm here." Jacob grinned proudly. "And he told me that though you're a student, he can get the best seats in the stadium for you, even for the away games."

"Great." I hoped my voice hadn't fallen flat. I hated going to football games. If I left to get a drink or go to the bathroom and missed something, Jacob would complain the whole damn night. As the alpha heir, he needed the perfect attentive mate, but he didn't seem to care that it wasn't me.

Beth smiled beside me, confirming my voice had in fact sounded less than enthusiastic.

All of the buildings were made of brick, and the Student Center was the largest. As we entered the building, we stepped right into an open area of bench seats against the walls and tables throughout. There had to be at least a hundred tables, and half of them were already filled.

"They're over here." Jacob tugged my hand, guiding us over to four tables that had been pushed together, and at least fifteen tall, huge guys were sitting around them.

They all smelled human. Jacob had told me there were very few wolves on the team. I guessed the others couldn't make it.

"Hey, there's our quarterback," Scott called out,

pointing right at Jacob. He was the largest of all fifteen and sat right in the center of the group. His dark hair was short, and his almost black eyes landed on me. "Damn, Emma. You got hotter since this summer."

He was a nice guy, if not a little overbearing; though he loved commenting on my looks. Sometimes, it made me feel dirty.

I'd met everyone on the team when I'd visited Jacob here for a day over summer. I'd wanted to get more acclimated to my surroundings.

"She's always been this beautiful." Jacob beamed widely as he tugged me against him and wrapped his arm around my waist. He bent down and kissed my lips.

I hated public displays of affection, but I couldn't pull away, especially not in front of his teammates. He wasn't doing anything wrong. In this case, 'it's not you, it's me' rang true.

"And this is her roommate, Beth." Jacob pointed at the girl on my other side.

"Hey." She eyed each player as if they were a treat.

"How have you been?" Scott focused back on me. "Are you trying out for cheer? I won't lie, it'd be a nice view for when I'm off the field."

A low growl came from the back of Jacob's throat, and his brown eyes glowed faintly.

That was one thing a wolf couldn't allow. When they viewed someone as their potential mate, they were possessive. I should have found that flattering, but I didn't. It annoyed me more than anything.

"Oh shit," Beth said so quietly that only Jacob and I could hear.

"No, I'm not. I'm just doing Dance class." I had to do something fast. I wrapped my arms around his shoulders and turned him toward me. I stood on my tiptoes, and right before my lips touched his cheek, I said, "And stop being an ass."

When my lips touched his skin, his body began to relax, and he turned his head to kiss my lips. I wanted to pull back, but I stayed there a few minutes longer. He had to calm down.

"Damn, Jacob." Scott laughed. "I love giving you a hard time. You're so protective of her."

My blood buzzed inside, and soon it was thrumming like never before. I pulled back, and my eyes flicked straight to the doorway.

Someone tall, dark, and handsome was standing there. His golden eyes locked on mine. He paused before turning and heading right back out the door.

I blinked several times, trying to understand what I'd just seen. That guy had looked like an older version of Aidan.

Aidan

I FELT a tug toward the Student Center even though it was the last place I wanted to be. I needed to get back home to make sure the society didn't get alerted about *her*—the girl I'd foolishly given my heart to four years ago.

Every day, it hurt just as damn badly as that night. How was that even fucking possible? Every time I closed my eyes, I still saw her face. Those haunting gray eyes, that sexy as hell cleft chin, and those soft, plump, pink lips.

I'd chosen my family over her, but by doing so, I was

protecting her from them. That was the only reason that kept me away.

The sizzling of my skin startled me from my thoughts as I opened the door and entered the building. As soon as I stepped foot inside, an electrical storm slammed into me. My eyes snapped to the large group of tables filled with students and zeroed in on her.

Emma.

I blinked a couple of times because nothing made sense. Her lips were on someone else's. Someone else had his arms around her waist. My wolf growled and pushed me to go over and jerk her from that douche's arms.

I was at a loss.

She must have felt the same thing because she pulled away from the asshole, and her eyes met mine.

I should've known better than to follow that tug. That was how I'd met her six damn years ago. The only thing this told me was that I'd be forever drawn to her, which would only end in heartbreak over and over again.

CHAPTER THREE

Emma

Within an hour, I told Jacob I was exhausted and ready to head back to the dorm. I was tired of pretending I was engaged in the conversation. My eyes kept going back to the doorway.

It couldn't have been him. It had to have been a dream... or had it been a nightmare? I wasn't sure which one I'd consider. The thought both thrilled and terrified me.

"Let me get my girl back to her room." Jacob stood and picked up our trays.

"I can get—"

"Nope, it's my job." He leaned over, kissed my lips, and then walked away.

He always got more affectionate around others. I wasn't sure if he was forcing me to be affectionate since I couldn't turn him down, or if he was laying a claim in front of the others. Either way, it wasn't cool, but it was impolite to make a scene in public.

"Are you going to hang out with us more now that you're on campus?" Scott's attention was back on me.

"Yeah." Even if I didn't, I'd be forced to. Jacob already had all these parties and things lined up for us to go to together.

He crossed his arms. "You don't sound too excited."

"It's her first day here. Give her time to adjust." Beth tilted her head as she studied me.

His buddies chuckled at the burn. The thinner one, named Adam, punched Scott in the arm. His blue eyes sparkled. "Two girls not begging to hang out with us. I'm not sure I like it."

"Sorry, but partying and hanging out isn't my focus." I was here to earn my nursing degree and make myself into something.

"You've still gotta have fun." Scott lifted both hands.

"Yeah, we'll loosen her up," Beth vowed.

Jacob frowned at Scott as he came back over and took my hand. "Is everything okay?"

"Yup." I forced a smile, wanting to leave. "Just ready to go." I placed my hand on his chest, emphasizing to Scott that I wasn't available or interested in his shenanigans. Jacob was more than enough. If I was going to settle for anyone, it made sense for it to be him. My parents approved, and it would make our pack happy.

Jacob's eyes warmed to a rich chocolate brown. "Then, let's get going."

"Maybe I should stay here a little longer?" Beth worded it like a question.

They all thought we wanted to fool around. Did Jacob expect the same thing? Now, I wanted to sit back down and refuse to leave.

"You're more than welcome to come back with us." I really wanted her to and hoped she'd get the hint.

"Oh, okay then." She stood. "I didn't want to impose."

"It's your dorm too." I was banking on Prescott being in Jacob's. *I don't want to leave her alone with these guys. She doesn't know them, and I don't want to start off on the wrong foot with her.*

Jacob's face fell a little, but that was it. "See you later," he called over his shoulder as we headed to the door. *You're right. She's your new roommate, so we shouldn't leave her behind. Maybe we can find some time alone tomorrow.*

My stomach dropped. This was not how things were supposed to go. I wasn't ready.

Once we were outside, Beth's shoulders relaxed. "I'm glad you were okay with me leaving with you. Those guys are hot, but I'd rather not be the only female there. There's no telling what I'd have had to listen to."

"That's why I wanted you to come with us." I had almost said the real reason but caught myself in the nick of time.

"Yeah, they talk a big game." Jacob shook his head and took a deep breath. "They're harmless, though."

"What's your class schedule?" It would be nice to have a class or two with someone I know.

Beth held up a finger for each class. "I've got Composition One, Calculus, Biology, and Art. What about you two?"

"I have Precalculus, Chemistry, Composition, and Dance." I'd been a cheerleader back in high school, and I'd regretted it the whole time. My senior year, I'd wanted to quit, but the coach had begged me to stay. The team had been half wolf shifters, and we were more athletic than the human girls. The coach had had no clue about it, but she'd known I was one of her best. Jacob had asked me to try out for cheer here, but I wanted to blend in and maybe even fade into the background. It was easier that way.

"When's your Composition class?" Beth grinned and crossed her fingers.

"Monday, Wednesday, and Friday at nine."

Her face lit up, and she clapped her hands. "We have at least one class together."

"And I have Chemistry with my girl." Jacob winked at me.

"I'm assuming you mean the class?" Beth glanced at me out of the corner of her eye.

"Yeah, I am." Jacob chuckled, thinking she was trying to be funny.

I knew better. How had she already figured out that I wasn't in love with him?

We were walking through the courtyard back to the dorm when a tingle ran down my spine. I turned around but didn't see a damn thing out of the ordinary.

It was official. I was losing my mind.

Jacob's forehead lined with worry. "Hey, are you okay?"

Why was he always asking me that? "Yeah, sorry." I looked over my shoulder again. "I just have the heebie-jeebies. Must be nerves."

Beth shrugged as she followed my gaze back to the Student Center. "I don't feel anything."

"Me neither." Jacob squeezed my hand reassuringly. "It's been a crazy day, so it's probably just your nerves. I wouldn't read too much into it."

He was right, but that Aidan lookalike still had me rattled. It had to have been the lighting or something. It didn't make sense to run into him at a university and not back home where our packs lived right next door to each other. It had to have been stress or the unfamiliar surroundings.

"You're right." I forced my head forward. "I do need to call it an early night." It was getting dark. I pulled my phone from my jeans pocket. It was almost nine, and the sky was black. "It's crazy how today has already flown by."

"We had a four-hour drive to get here," Jacob said comfortingly. "That's why."

He had a point. "True."

When we reached the women's dorm, I turned to him and gave him a small smile. "Goodnight."

"Night." He brushed his lips with mine. When he pulled back, he ran his fingers through my hair. "I'll come by and grab you for lunch tomorrow after class."

"Okay, that sounds good." I walked to the door.

"See ya," Beth called as she followed me.

I'd expected her to bombard me with questions or comments, so her silence threw me. The lobby was full downstairs, and as we walked by, Caroline sat straight in the chair and called out, "Emma. Come join us."

Great, this was not what I wanted to do, but it would be rude to ignore her. "Hey." I forced my usual fake smile and grabbed Beth's arm when she tried to run off.

"Hey, they're talking to you, not me," Beth grumbled as my iron grasp didn't weaken.

Caroline huffed and smirked. She crossed her legs, her black miniskirt leaving little to the imagination, and crossed her arms over her chest, which emphasized her boobs in her white, low-cut shirt. She was sitting on a couch with Jules on the other end and two girls who looked like their clones sitting on the ground in front of them.

This was the last place I wanted to be. I'd just left high

school where I'd been forced to be around girls like them. "What's up?"

"How long have you and Jacob been together?" She bit her bottom lip, waiting for my answer.

Of course, this would be about him. "About two years. Why?"

"And he's still that in love with you?" She frowned as if she had hoped our relationship was a recent lustful thing.

"Apparently so." Beth laughed and looked off to the side.

"What's so funny?" Jules asked, frowning.

"That you think you have a chance." Beth rolled her eyes. "He doesn't see anyone else but her. I could tell that within the first five minutes."

"We also want to be her friend." Caroline lifted her hands as if in surrender and wrinkled her nose as if Beth smelled. Caroline patted the sofa in the spot between her and Jules. "Come join us."

I didn't feel like hanging out and making the same type of friends I had back home. This was supposed to be a fresh start, and I didn't want to be popular. "Nah, I'm good." I nodded toward Beth. "We're gonna go set up our room, but thanks for the invite." I turned my back to them and pointed to the stairwell. "Let's go."

"Yeah, okay." She smiled, almost taken aback by what I'd done.

"Oh, well. Maybe tomorrow?" Caroline sounded unsure.

"We'll see." Being part of the in-crowd wasn't all it was cracked up to be. Most of them were living their glory days. They'd peak early and either land a rich husband or always believe they were worth more than they actually were.

That's the main lesson Aidan had taught me. We were disposable, and I was nothing special.

As we reached the stairwell, Caroline whispered, "Why'd she choose that weirdo over us?"

They didn't think we could hear, but we could.

Beth's eyes flashed with anger as she paused.

"They aren't worth it." I grabbed her arm and tugged her toward the steps. "Let's go get some rest. Tomorrow is a brand new day."

ALL NIGHT, I tossed and turned. Every time I closed my eyes, his face popped into my head. At first, he looked the same as the last time I'd seen him over four years ago; then he morphed into the man I saw today. I could still visualize the gold flecks in his eyes and smell his piney scent.

Finally, my alarm went off. I was tired, but at least now, I would have a distraction. My mind wouldn't keep wandering back to him.

"Damn, you're a morning person," Beth mumbled as she grabbed her pillow and put it over her head.

"I didn't sleep much last night, so I'm ready to get this day going." I walked over to the small closet we shared and pulled out a teal dress. It was my favorite color, and I needed something to cheer me up.

"Why not?" She threw the pillow aside and sat up. "Worried about Caroline going after Jacob?"

"What? No." That wasn't a concern, and it had nothing to do with my confidence. Shifters weren't allowed to date outside of their race. It complicated things.

"Hmm..." Her blue eyes examined me.

"Okay, I'm going to take a shower and get ready." I

didn't need someone trying to figure me out. That was one of the nice things about Libby and Grace. They only worried about themselves, so I was in the clear most of the time. I put on my robe and headed out the door.

After grabbing a bite at the Student Center, Beth and I rushed up the stairs to the third floor. We got to Composition One with ten minutes to spare.

"Look like we have our choice of seats." Beth threw her wrapper into the garbage while balancing her cup of coffee and picked a desk at the very back. "Sit in front of me so I don't have to smell the humans the entire time."

"What about me having to?" I didn't mind, but I had to give her a hard time over it.

"I'll owe you one." She pouted at me and lowered her head, which reminded me of a puppy dog. She had the look down pat.

She was not afraid to be herself, which made me respect her more. "Do you think that actually works on people?" I was already warming up to her, and that kind of scared me. It'd been so long since I'd let someone in.

"Yup, because you are already taken in by my charm." She sipped her coffee.

"What charm?" I wanted to challenge her, but she was still mopey, "Fine," I said as I plopped into the seat, pretending to be upset. I wasn't, but I couldn't let her think she'd won so easily.

Other students soon trickled in. The first ones stayed away from us. Humans naturally distanced themselves from us, even though they didn't understand why. Supernaturals were predators. Hell, even witches were. Though our species was alluring, we also made humans feel uncomfortable.

"Did you already get your books?" Beth leaned over her desk and spoke a little louder than a whisper.

"Yeah, I did." The spots in the front were filling up, and soon, only one spot was left—the one right beside Beth in the very back.

Beth groaned. "I'll have to go after my classes."

Something changed in the air, and my skin buzzed.

No, this couldn't be happening.

Powerless, my eyes went straight to the door as the tall, dark, and handsome man entered.

It was almost like we were magnets because his eyes locked on mine at the exact same time.

His eyes glowed before he looked away in search of an open seat.

No... God, please no. I couldn't have him this close.

Ugh, I was being stupid. There was no way he could be the boy I loved. He was too rugged, too hardened. His body was tense like he didn't want to come toward me, and his chiseled face was sexy as hell.

The closer in proximity to me he came, the more my body hummed. As he brushed past me, the piney scent I had burned into my memory hit me like a freight train.

I wanted to run, but there was nowhere far enough to fix my already fracturing heart.

CHAPTER FOUR

Aidan

Her gray eyes locked on mine, and I knew she felt everything I did. Her mouth dropped open, and her breathing quickened. Judging by her reaction to me, there was no way she was in love with that guy.

But it didn't matter. She was my target and nothing more. I had to remember that.

I should've left the class right then and there, but my legs propelled me toward her. My heart didn't give a damn that I needed to stay away. I guessed it loved the torture of being near her and not having her.

As I passed her, the sweet vanilla scent hit me right in the gut. She wasn't a girl anymore but a smoking hot woman. Her eyes looked haunted, and it hurt to think I'd caused her pain. I pushed the thought away. It didn't matter. My choices were best for both of us.

Her friend watched me as I approached; her interest in me evident in her eyes. She was cute, but not Emma. No girl was, and no one would ever be. I would make sure they both stayed away.

Emma

I DIDN'T KNOW what the hell to do. He was so close. I could smell his signature scent with each breath. The problem was that his scent was better than I remembered it. The memory of it had faded more than I'd realized. There was no question, whether this was Aidan or not, he was a shifter.

"Hey there, handsome," Beth cooed.

He didn't respond, and the tickling feeling in the back of my spine took over again. It was as if his eyes were locked on me.

"Oh, she's taken." Beth moved, and it sounded like she'd turned her body toward him. "I'm not."

Once again, the guy didn't answer her.

Maybe I was wrong. Aidan wouldn't be that rude. Maybe he was a doppelganger or something. I wasn't sure if that would make the situation better or not, but I couldn't let hope fill me again. I almost hadn't survived him. When he'd left me, he'd taken a part of me with him that I'd never get back.

"Are you deaf?" Beth's tone was now annoyed.

"Not interested." His voice was deep and low, heating my body.

I had to get myself under control before anyone noticed what he was doing to me.

Right as I was about to stand and run, the professor walked in, and class began.

CLASS CRAWLED BY. I couldn't listen to a damn thing the professor said as my focus was on the person seated behind me on the left.

It wasn't just me struggling. He had a hard time paying attention too. His pencil kept hitting the desk over and over again, a fidgeting motion that held my attention. When I'd shift in my seat, the tapping would increase.

God, I was a narcissist. It wasn't like he was focused on me like I was on him. I was losing my mind.

As soon as class ended, I jumped to my feet and practically ran out the door.

"Emma," Beth yelled as she followed behind, "wait up."

I didn't want to slow down, but people were stopping in the hallway to watch.

It was hard as hell to slow down, but I planted my feet. As I turned around to face Beth, I prayed, *Please don't let him be there.*

"What is wrong with you?" Beth rushed to me and glanced around at the people watching as if they expected us to fight.

Of course, Aidan was a few steps back, his attention on me.

Why did he keep looking at me? I felt fourteen years old again. I wanted to throw a tantrum right here in the middle of the busy hallway.

"Sorry, just so worried about my next class." I took a deep, calming breath and laughed a little too loudly. I was officially acting weird.

"Your class is in this building." She pointed to the stairs. "On the first floor."

It was time to reel it in. I huffed and closed my eyes for a moment. "You're right. It's just nerves. I was thinking the building was across campus, but that's tomorrow's classes."

"My class is actually a few buildings over, so I have to go." Her forehead was creased with worry. "You sure you're okay?"

"Promise." No, no I wasn't, but she didn't need my shit dumped on her. No one knew about Aidan. I'd never told Libby or Grace. The less I talked about it, the better.

"Okay, I'll meet up with you in a couple of hours." She paused before turning and heading to the stairs.

"See ya." The crowd had dispersed, and no one was paying me any attention.

I pushed my legs forward and headed to the first floor for Precalculus. My phone buzzed in my backpack, so I paused outside the classroom and pulled it out.

Hey, Babe—Hope your first few classes are going well. See you soon. <3

Even though I didn't love him like I'd loved Aidan, he was loyal, dependable, and crazy about me. That counted for something. It had to.

I sat at the very back and smoothed out my dress as I crossed my legs. I was getting ready to respond to Jacob's text when the piney scent hit me all over again.

I glanced up and found the same guy sitting right next to me.

"Is that your boyfriend or something?" His sexy voice caressed my ears.

"Uh... a friend." The words were out, and I couldn't take them back. I should have just said yes. "I... mean, yeah." My eyes flicked at his, and it was like I was paralyzed.

He arched an eyebrow. "Which one is it?"

Wrong move. I needed to abort my gaze before I started

drooling, but dammit, I couldn't. "One what?" Smooth. Real smooth, Emma. But could this really be Aidan?

"Do you have a boyfriend or not?" His eyes moved to my lips.

And, I licked them inadvertently.

Aidan

HER TONGUE WAS DOING awful things to me, and she wasn't even trying. I shouldn't have been flirting or showing any interest, but I couldn't stop myself. When I'd spied the message, it had made me want to scream and punch someone, so I'd let my guard down with her.

I was only making it harder on us. I needed to stop, but for some god-awful reason, I couldn't.

"All right." The professor entered the classroom and clapped his hands. "Who's ready for math?" It effectively cut off our conversation.

Emma

MATH WAS something I couldn't fall behind on, so thankfully, I was forced to keep my attention elsewhere. I enjoyed numbers, so time flew by, and before I realized it, class was over.

My body stiffened, and I took a deep breath. I had this. All I needed to do was pack up my books and walk out the door. It couldn't be that hard. I'd never struggled with it before.

I zipped up my bag, threw it over my shoulder, and headed out the door. Luckily, he hadn't said anything, so my escape was easy.

Outside the building, I sucked in the fresh air, trying to forget his all-too-tantalizing smell.

"Emma," Jacob called out, and I turned to find him and Scott heading my way.

"Oh, hey." I hadn't expected to run into him here. He still had one more class. "What are you doing here?"

"My last class is in this building." He smiled as he reached me.

"Right." His last class was Composition II, so it made sense for him to be here. I looked over my shoulder, hoping that guy wasn't out here. "Gotcha. I'm done for the day."

"Yup. You want me to swing by and get you on the way to the Student Center?" He lowered his head and tried to kiss my lips.

Fearing that Aidan was behind me and watching, I moved out of the way. Dammit, I wasn't being fair, and I'd hear about it tonight from Jacob. "Or I can meet you there if it's easier."

"Yeah, meet us there." Scott nodded, but his brows furrowed. "Maybe you could get there before the lunch crowd and save us a few seats. There should be about six of us."

"Sure, I can do that." I pulled him into a hug as my skin buzzed. I needed to get away. "See you soon."

I hurried toward the dorm, needing a few minutes to myself.

I RAN to my room within minutes and slammed the door.

Beth dropped her backpack to the ground and turned around. "Are you on something?" She looked at me as if I had two heads.

I'd expected to beat her here, so I probably looked crazy, especially considering the way I'd hurried out of the first class.

"Let me start by saying you are not normal." She snorted and sat on her bed, watching me.

Under these circumstances, I had to agree with her there.

"It was after that smoking hot guy—" She paused and pointed at me. "—shifter entered that classroom."

"What?" My voice sounded strangely high, and I winced. "No." I waved my hand out toward her and flung my backpack on the ground.

"Right..." She leaned back on her elbows. "That's what you're going with."

For the first time in my life, I wanted to tell someone everything. It was crazy. I'd known her only about twenty-four hours, but she didn't hate his pack and wouldn't judge me like the others.

"Look, I get it." She tilted her head in my direction. "You don't know me that well, but you can smell a lie. And I promise, if you tell me anything, I won't say a word."

"Why do you think there's something wrong?" *Other than me acting like a nutcase*, I wanted to add, but I didn't.

"Let's see. You started acting strange right around the time big, dark, and broody entered the room." She bounced her leg. "And he stared at you so hard I was surprised laser beams didn't shoot out and kill you."

"He was staring at me?" No, stop. I couldn't let myself hope. He'd left me. "He reminds me of someone I used to know, but I'm not sure it's him."

"Yeah... so what's the story?" She sat straight up and pointed at her bag. "You'd be helping me. I don't feel like studying right now."

"I've never told anyone." It sounded so ominous.

She slapped the bed. "That's usually how the best stories go."

"I found my first love six years ago. We were drawn to the boundary line one day." I didn't want to get into my whole backstory about being adopted. That wasn't the point. "We stared at each other for a few minutes before he finally said, 'Hi.' That's when things clicked, and we became fast friends."

"So, you got to play with each other?"

"Oh, no. Our packs aren't friendly." All other packs were okay for us to intermingle with if I found someone or even my fated, but not his. "We had to stay on our own side of the line."

She pursed her lips. "That sucks."

"A few months before my fourteenth birthday, things changed between us." I had seen him in a new light. "He was handsome, kind, and understood me more than anyone else ever had."

She stayed quiet, which surprised me.

"The night before my fourteenth birthday, he told me he felt the same way. He'd handmade me a necklace." It was kind of embarrassing. I had the damn necklace here with me in my jewelry box. "We kissed that night." I rubbed my finger along my lips, pretending they were his lips. "Everything was perfect until he put my necklace on me. Then, he rushed away. We were supposed to meet the next night, but he never showed up at our spot again."

"Wait... what?" Her mouth opened. "He just disappeared after giving you a present and that kiss?"

"Yeah, I don't know what I did." It had haunted me since. I'd tried to find out what had caused him to leave me behind, and it always came back to the necklace, which didn't make any damn sense.

"So, that guy is him?" She glanced out the window as if expecting to see him there.

"I don't know." I plopped down on my bed and frowned. "He looks like him, and the piney scent is exactly the same."

"Scent doesn't lie." She lay on her side, keeping her eyes on me. "So... I'm thinking it's him."

"Then maybe I should go back home." I blew out a breath. "I'm here with Jacob, and I don't need Aidan complicating things again."

"What?" She rolled over, stood from the bed, and joined me on mine. "No. First off, you have a boyfriend. That shows you've moved on even if it's not true. And two, this is an opportunity to find out why he left you and get closure."

"And get my heart broken again?" I couldn't allow that to happen.

"Oh, hell no." She took my hand in hers. "That won't happen."

"Because I have Jacob now." He was everything a wolf shifter could want in her mate... except me.

"Besides, we both know you only love him as a friend, and let's be real; he's a little off. I haven't quite put my finger on it yet." She looked at me from the top of her eyes. "And don't lie to me. You're still hung up on that guy. This may be the tipping point that will make you feel the same way about Jacob as you do him."

"It was four years ago. I was a young girl." Sometimes, I still felt that way, but the experience had made me stronger. "But you're right."

"It's the lack of closure that's your problem." She bumped her shoulder into mine. "We've got this."

"No, no." I pointed my finger at her. "I have to move on." Maybe this was a test to see if I had really left the pain all behind.

"Fine, we'll try it your way." She shrugged a shoulder and sighed. "At least, at first."

I grabbed my phone to look at the time. "Oh, shit. I told Jacob and Scott I'd go grab some tables before their class got out. You want to join me?"

"Uh, yeah. Football players and food." Beth stood and winked. "I'm all for the combination, and that allows me to put off studying for a little longer."

"Okay, let's go."

We reached the Student Center within minutes. It was around eleven-thirty, and the place was filling up with the lunch crowd.

We snagged a corner section and pulled three tables up to make room for twelve. I'd learned that more football players often appeared than anticipated.

"There she is," Jacob said as he headed straight to me. He pulled me into his arms and kissed my forehead. "I see you planned for extras."

"She knows how we roll." Scott chuckled and threw his bag into one of the chairs. "Why don't you three go grab some food, and I'll hold down the fort until another one shows up."

My stomach growled, which made Jacob smile. "Sounds like Emma agrees."

"Oh, shut it." I smacked him on the chest, trying to prevent the grin from spreading across my face.

"Let's go before you get more violent." He grabbed my hand and tugged me behind him.

These times got me through and provided a glimmer of happiness even if it was short-lived. Jacob did have a way of making me smile. I only wished my heart felt more for him.

"You turd."

"Oh, I love the way you talk dirty to me." He laughed and wrapped his arm around my waist.

It didn't take us long before we had our lunch and joined the others at the table. However, I had a hard time paying attention to the conversation around me as I picked at my burger.

A piney scent hit my nose, and I stupidly glanced behind me.

There he was yet again today. His eyes were locked on the arm around my waist, and his jaw was clenched.

Looking forward, I forced myself not to look behind me again at Aidan or not-Aidan; that's where I needed to leave my past.

CHAPTER FIVE

The next morning, I stood in line with Jacob for breakfast.

"I'm so glad we have Chemistry together even if I hate science." Jacob paid for our food at the Student Center, his eyes bright. "We've never had one together."

"You do realize, for a business degree, you could've taken Biology or something else." I wanted to be a registered nurse so this was one class I had to take. It helped that I enjoyed all sciences in general.

"True, but I needed a science course, and you were taking one." He shrugged as we headed over to the group of football players who had saved us a seat. "Gave me an incentive to get that on my schedule."

"Even with the lab right after on Thursdays?" He hated science, so Biology might have been a better choice for him.

"Yup. I have a feeling I'll get the best lab partner the school can provide." He set the tray on the table. "But I'll need tutoring."

"Oh, I'm sure you will." I took my coffee and egg-bacon biscuit off the tray. I unwrapped the biscuit and took a huge bite. Last night, I hadn't eaten much, so my stomach was upset and yelling at me... well, in all fairness, it was more gurgling. I needed the calories since my nine a.m. class was Dance.

I'd closed my eyes, enjoying the salty taste of bacon, when that damn scent hit me again, and I choked on my bite. I hadn't smelled it in years, and now I couldn't go anywhere without it popping up.

"Emma." Jacob turned toward me and started hitting my back.

"No, I'm fine." What he was doing was making it worse. I grabbed my coffee and took a large sip. The liquid burned my throat as it went down. I coughed more, but luckily, the food had dislodged. "Give me a second."

"You might need to give her mouth to mouth." Scott shook his head as he sat across from Jacob.

"He..." I coughed again. "... probably doesn't want to do that." My last word was cut off again, and I took another swig of coffee.

"Why don't you drink some of my water instead of scalding your throat?" Jacob handed me the bottle, and I gladly drank out of it.

"Thank you." Eyes watering, I glanced at a table placed two away from us and found the Aidan lookalike sitting there. Our eyes met, and my skin buzzed. "Let me go get another one for you."

"No, it's fine." Jacob lifted his hands. "I can grab another one later. It's no big deal."

"I insist." I needed to clear the air... literally. I jumped to my feet and rushed past the one person I was way too aware of. Out of range of his scent, I took a deep breath, but the smell hadn't gone away.

"It's a bad sign when you have to run away from your boyfriend."

I stopped in my tracks and turned around. His soulful eyes looked at me. A small smile played at the corner of his lips, and his fitted black shirt emphasized his muscles.

He nibbled on his bottom lip. "Not going to deny it?"

The nibbling was Aidan's tic. "What?" In the last conversation we'd had, I'd said the very same thing. I couldn't allow this asshole to mess with my mind. "No, I choked and drained half of Jacob's water, so I'm getting him a new one."

"So, he is your boyfriend?" he asked. Something flashed in his eyes. I thought it might be anger, but it disappeared before I could confirm it.

"Why does it matter to you?" I tried controlling my breathing as I waited for the answer. It was fucking ridiculous. This person had affected me way too much in a matter of days.

"It shouldn't," he breathed, but he took a step closer to me.

The words felt like a slap across the face, but at least, he was honest.

"But it does," he rasped, which almost made me think I'd imagined them.

Almost.

"You feel the same way." He reached his hand out as if to brush my cheek with his fingertips. "I smell your attraction."

I nodded before I could stop myself. This had to be Aidan.

Aidan

I WAS BEING RECKLESS. I shouldn't have been following her, but I couldn't stop myself. I was turning into a stalker.

Her affirmation that she was attracted to me was making me lose my mind. My hand was only millimeters from her skin, and dammit, I wanted to feel her and taste her. It'd been too damn long.

Every ounce of self-control... of my conviction to do the right thing and walking away left me. I was about to take her in my arms and kiss away all the doubt and concern.

Then, he appeared and ruined it all.

Emma

"BABE?" Jacob's voice brought me back down to earth. "What's going on?" His gaze zeroed in on Aidan's fingers, which were only a few millimeters from my face.

"He was checking on me." I forced a cough again. "And was brushing biscuit off my face." Wow, I was a horrible liar and hoped the smells of the food covered the scent of my lie.

"Oh, okay." Jacob stepped beside me, took my hand, and pulled me a few steps away from Aidan and next to him. "Thanks, man. I got it from here." *He's attracted to you.*

I'm sure it's something else. This was so fucking awkward.

No, the scent is loud and clear. His eyes were locked on Aidan's, and it was obvious they were in a pissing match.

"Yeah, okay." Aidan's jaw clenched, and he took a deep breath and headed back out to the seating area.

"Babe, you should've just linked me." Jacob's eyes softened. "I would've been here in an instant. You don't need to put up with someone pestering you like that."

"Oh, I know, but I didn't want to bother you." That wasn't a lie, so I was safe with those words.

"You come before everything." He smiled softly. "I'm not sure how much more I can prove that."

"You don't have to prove anything." We hadn't had one of these conversations in over a year. I always felt bad because he knew how much he gave and how little I returned despite how hard I tried. I knew my parents and his dad wanted us to work out.

"Look, let's get another bottle of water and finish our breakfast." I kissed his cheek and let go of his hand. Giving him extra attention should get him to lay off me. "No reason for both of our food to get cold."

He growled, clearly not ready to drop it. The jealousy radiated off him like crazy.

Nope, not happening. I wouldn't allow him to press it this time. I walked off, leaving him behind.

"Emma," he whined and hurried to catch up to me. And just like that, he caved... for once.

I WALKED out of the locker room after changing out of my dance clothes and found Jacob waiting by the door.

"Hey, you." I smiled at him. I was in a good mood now. This was the first time I'd taken Dance in years, and I'd loved every second. Cheerleading had replaced Dance for way too long. The coach had asked me to try out for the university's dance squad, but I hadn't wanted to. I just wanted to have fun and not tie myself down to anything.

"You seem awfully happy." He took my backpack from me.

I hated when he did that. It's like he thought I couldn't carry a damn bag. Mom used to get on me, telling me that's how gentlemen were raised and I should be thankful I had someone so attentive. I focused on what mattered. "I haven't taken a class for fun in so long. It feels really nice."

"I'm glad." He took my hand and squeezed it. "I thought you were making a mistake by not doing cheer, but you seem really happy."

That was the point. To find things that made me happy. I'd almost forgotten what happiness was like until this class. At times, it felt like I was just apathetic. Nothing more.

We walked across the greenway. When we'd pass the other football players, they'd bump fists with Jacob, and a few girls frowned when they saw our joined hands.

I couldn't blame them.

"After class, I'll have a couple of hours to eat and do some work before heading to practice." We walked toward the science building across from the English department. "So maybe we can eat lunch and head to the library."

I had to catch up on what I hadn't paid attention to in English and do some math work. "Sounds good to me."

"Great." He stepped closer to me as we passed by a larger group.

"Oh, Jacob." A girl turned around and raced back to us. Her hazel eyes looked at our joined hands, giving her pause. "Uh...we're having a party Friday night that you're invited to."

"Just me?" He lifted our joined hands.

This was where he differed from most guys. He was making it a point to ensure I wasn't excluded and showing that he was taken.

"I thought you had a girlfriend back home." Her light blonde hair bounced as she shrugged. "So..."

"This is my girlfriend from back home." He laughed and pulled me closer to wrap an arm around me. "I wouldn't be holding hands with anyone else."

"Of course she'd go here." Disappointment was clear in her words. "She's invited too."

"I'm right here." I was used to human girls falling all over themselves for Jacob.

"Uh... yeah." She rolled her eyes and forced a giggle. "So you can come too."

"We'll think about it." Jacob tugged me forward. "We've gotta get going or we'll miss class. See you later."

Once we were close to our building, I winced. "Do you want to go to that party?" I really didn't want to, but I'd go for him.

"Nah, we have our first game this weekend, so we need to rest and not end up hungover." He rolled his eyes. "It's not against one of the better teams, but it's at noon, and we'll be getting up early for warm-ups. I was thinking we could go off campus to eat and watch a movie."

"That sounds more like my speed." I hated being around a lot of people. All those fake smiles and forced laughter were tiring me out.

"I know." He adjusted the backpack on his shoulder. "And you should invite your roommate. Since Prescott is a wolf and you and Beth get along so well, I was thinking we could go on a double date."

He was right. Hanging out with a couple would be fun, and that would be less alone time with Jacob. "That would be nice."

Jacob opened the door to the building for me, and the

smell of chemicals burned my nose as we entered the hallway.

He wrinkled his nose and blew out a breath. "Ugh... sometimes I wish I didn't have a sensitive nose."

"Stop being dramatic." I smacked him on the arm. "You'll get used to it in a few minutes."

"I'm not so sure about that." He headed to a door, and I followed behind him.

I stepped into the room and stopped. There he was again. How the hell did we have three classes together?

There were only two open seats, and they were across the room from one another. I'd known we would be getting here later, but I hadn't expected to run into this issue.

"Yo, Jacob." Adam from the football team waved and pointed to the empty seat beside him. "Since you two can't sit together, might as well sit with me."

Jacob frowned when he saw who I'd be sitting next to. *I don't want you sitting next to him.*

I didn't blame him, but dammit... I wasn't disappointed like I should have been. I was thrilled, which was the whole fucking problem. He still had power over me after all this time. *I can sit with Adam.*

"Come on, man," Adam hollered again.

No, I'll look like an ass if I don't sit with him. Jacob huffed and headed over to where Aidan sat and put my bag down.

Aidan watched him and smirked.

It was obvious how much Jacob didn't like it.

"There you go." He brushed his lips against mine.

My hand fisted, but I didn't pull away. It would cause a fight if I did, and I didn't have the energy for it. It surprised me when I heard a very faint growl from Aidan.

Jacob sighed and headed over to his friend, Adam.

As I slipped into my seat, I felt both sets of eyes on me. I had to ignore them both. Class would be starting any second.

Aidan

I'D RESOLVED yesterday to be cold and distant. That's what would get us both through this evaluation that my pack had sent me here for.

But the moment that arrogant asshole came in, staking her as his, it pissed me off. She wasn't property. He was a controlling, manipulative asshole.

He might be an alpha's son, but so was I. I should have gotten up and left, headed back to Mount Juliet and told them I'd taken care of her, but my brother had let it slip that an ally was here. Until I could determine who it was, I was stuck here, pretending to still be scouting her out.

Maybe if I pointed out that she wasn't happy, it would make things easier on us. She was a smart woman, but she didn't see how much she was worth.

Emma

"IT ISN'T a good sign when your boyfriend kisses you and you make a fist," he said so lightly I barely heard him.

Sitting next to Aidan wasn't going to be good. Jacob and I would have to figure out a way to sit together on Thursday. "It's none of your business."

"It's not?" He arched an eyebrow.

"Just stop." I glared at him. "Let's cut the shit. Why are you here?"

"Well, I thought it was pretty obvious." He twirled his finger, indicating the building. "An education."

"Aidan." I had to confirm it was him.

"Emma." He leaned toward me, his scent sending my hormones into overdrive.

Okay, it was worse now. It really was him. There was no more pretending.

Emma? Jacob linked with me. *Are you okay? Is he bothering you?*

I winced and looked forward. *No, I'm fine.*

You don't look fine. Jacob had stood from his seat when the professor entered the room.

"Sorry I'm late." The older man's gray hair was in complete disarray, and he hurried to the front of the class. "Now, let's begin."

CLASS WAS WINDING DOWN, and I was at my wit's end. Aidan hadn't even pretended to take notes, and I'd struggled to pay attention since he was right beside me. I was aware of every time he took a breath, when his attention was on me, and the times he fidgeted. He'd brushed his arm against mine five times, causing the buzzing of my skin to reach levels I'd never experienced before.

"So... the last thing to address." The professor placed a hand in his pocket and then lifted his other in the air and gestured across the room. "These are your seats for this semester, and your table mate is your lab partner. Please exchange phone numbers or email addresses in case something happens and you can't make it to class." He removed his hand from his pocket and rubbed his hands together and then dropped them to his sides. "Class dismissed. Remember to look over the next chapter and read through the lab work for Thursday. The more prepared you are, the better.

Whoa. Now I was stuck with him as a lab partner. I refused to accept those terms.

I stood from my seat, and Jacob was beside me in a flash.

"Hey, man." Jacob nodded at Aidan. "How about we switch spots on Thursday? Adam's good at science."

"He said these were our seats for the rest of the semester." Aidan's eyes lightened.

"Well, yeah, but I'm sure if we change next time, it won't be a biggie." Jacob grabbed my bag and put it on his arm.

"No, sorry." Aidan ripped a piece of paper from his notebook and scribbled his number on it with a black pen. He ripped the bottom section off and handed it to me with the pen. "I'll need your number, too, like the professor said."

"He has a..." I started but stopped. Aidan almost seemed hurt.

I schooled my expression into a mask of indifference and wrote down my number. "Fine, here."

"Emma." Jacob's surprised voice hit me in the gut.

"It's fine." I grabbed the piece of paper with Aidan's number on it, folded it up, and put it in my bag. "It's just one lousy class and lab. It's not worth fighting over."

"You're right, but..." Jacob switched to our mind link. *I don't like the way he's looking at you.*

There's nothing to worry about. I forced my hand to reach for Jacob's. *Let's go eat some lunch.*

Jacob nodded, and we headed to the door. I could still feel Aidan's eyes on me.

Without thinking about it, I glanced over my shoulder. Our eyes locked, and my heart skipped a beat. Aidan attending school here was going to change everything.

Aidan

I WAS PLAYING WITH FIRE. Emma should've held her ground and forced me to switch seats, but she hadn't.

However, when she'd said my name—damn, it had been like a drink of water after a long drought.

The fact she'd given me her number even though that prick hadn't been thrilled gave me false hope. I had to get my head on straight. We would both get hurt or killed if we continued down this road.

But I needed her number for class. The professor had made us exchange numbers, and I'd given mine in return. I pulled out my phone and quickly typed out a text. I knew I shouldn't send it, but when did I ever play by anyone else's rules?

CHAPTER SIX

Emma

"I don't like that guy," Jacob grumbled as we left the classroom.

It took everything I had not to turn around and look at Aidan again. I'd honestly almost convinced myself it wasn't him. Yeah, stupid, but it was me trying to survive. Knowing it was him made a huge difference, which pissed me off. He'd left me. Why in the world had he popped up now?

"Did he say something to you?" Jacob squeezed my hand, bringing me back down to reality.

"Huh?" It wouldn't help things if he knew I wasn't listening.

Jacob paused. "I asked if he said something to you."

"Oh, no." I shook my head hard.

"You do realize I can smell your lie, right?" Jacob growled and pulled me to a stop. "What did he say?"

I would have to tell him. He deserved to know the truth. "Look, I know him."

"What? How?" Jacob glanced at the ground, and he

pursed his lips. That was his tell when he was trying to figure something out and wasn't happy.

"He's part of the Murphy pack." This wouldn't go over well.

His eyes jerked to mine. "Back home?"

"Yeah." I didn't want to get into all the details yet. I needed to work through my feelings before I told him everything.

"Wait, we don't interact with them." He rubbed a hand down his neck and displeasure radiated through our mind link. "How did you meet him?"

"We ran across each other by chance." I shrugged. "We were kids."

"Okay..." He blew out a breath, and his jaw clenched. "Why didn't you tell me in the cafeteria when you saw him?"

I was getting angry, so I had to keep my calm or he'd realize there was more to the story. "I hadn't seen him in over four years. I didn't know it was him until we talked in Chemistry."

His shoulders sagged. "Good. For a second, I was afraid you were keeping things from me."

"No, it just shocked me. He doesn't look like the boy I knew, so it threw me."

"There's my roomie," Beth called loudly.

Thank God. I needed to get out of this awkward conversation and quickly.

"Is there trouble in paradise?" Beth arched an eyebrow as her eyes bounced between Jacob and me.

"No." Jacob shook his head, but a frown marred his face. "Apparently, someone from back home is here and causing problems. I shouldn't be surprised with him being a Murphy and all."

"Someone from back home." She mashed her lips together and huffed. "Interesting."

Her face screamed, 'You'd better tell me everything soon.' It wouldn't be an issue since I needed to talk to someone, and she was the only person who knew everything.

"We're heading to grab lunch before going to the library." His usual good-guy demeanor returned. "Want to join us?"

"Sounds great." She grinned, and the three of us headed toward the Student Center.

Beth, Jacob, and I got situated at a table in the library, and as I pulled out my books, my phone vibrated. I glanced at the number but didn't recognize it.

Enjoy your time with Lover Boy.

No, it couldn't be.

I put my bag on the floor to fish out the number Aidan had given me. I looked at the paper and back at my phone, and it sunk in. Yeah, it was definitely him.

There was no way in hell I was responding to that. He'd ignored me for four years; it was his turn to see how it felt.

"Emma? Are you okay?" Jacob's gaze landed on my phone.

"Oh, yeah." I stuffed the paper back into the small pocket of my bag and tossed my phone on the table. "Just distracted." That was the total truth there. I pulled out my English book and set it on the table.

The three of us hunkered down and began working.

About an hour later, Jacob lifted his arms in a stretch. "I'd better head back to the dorm to get ready for football practice."

"Okay." I kept my focus on my textbook. I'd read the same sentence at least a hundred times. My eyes kept getting drawn to my damn phone.

"I should be done around six." He kissed my lips. "I'll drop by and get you."

I nodded, trying not to frown. It would be nice to have one evening not dominated by him. At least, when he'd gone to college back home, he hadn't come over for dinner every night. He'd come over most nights, but his parents wanted him home some, too.

"See you." Beth waved as he headed to the door. "Okay." She stood and took over Jacob's spot. "Ew, it's warm."

"Well, he just left." I needed the laugh. "So... kind of your fault."

"Oh, shush." She moved so she was close to me.

The tables around us were pretty much empty except for two people working on a project five tables over.

"Jacob wasn't his warm, carefree self." Beth pointed to her ear. "So let me have it."

"So, the guy who reminded me of my first love..." I still couldn't believe it myself.

"Yes..." She grabbed my arm and widened her eyes. "Tell me before I have to kick your ass."

"Patience." I hoped to be able to say it straight up. "It's him."

"What?" She leaned back and touched my arm as her mouth dropped open. "No way. How are you sure?"

I filled her in on everything that had happened earlier.

Her eyes widened. "So, why were you acting strange when we first got here?"

"He sent me this text." I unlocked the phone and showed her.

"Wow. He has some balls and called Jacob Lover Boy also." She shook her head. "Are you going to respond?"

"No, he can kiss my ass." The more I thought about it, the more pissed I became.

"I agree, girl." She fidgeted in her chair and nodded. "He's damn fine and smells like heaven, but he did you wrong."

"Yes, he did." There wasn't much more to say than that.

THE NEXT MORNING, Beth and I were the first ones in the classroom for Composition. We took our normal seats in the back, and my heart began racing.

Aidan

I'D WAITED by my phone all night for Emma to text me back, but I got nothing. I deserved it, but damn. She was probably with him. God knew what they were doing... All the possibilities made me want to vomit.

I grabbed my bag and headed out the door, slamming it shut. Luckily, I'd gotten a room to myself. My roommate hadn't shown at the last second, which was for the best.

Normally, I'd head to get breakfast, but I wasn't hungry. I was just so angry. At her, but not at her. It wasn't her fault. It wasn't like she'd chosen our connection, but dammit, I was going crazy, and she could've at least texted me something back.

That was it. I had to stop being friendly. We were playing a dangerous game. I needed to let my anger and pain fuel me from here on out.

Emma

"You'd better be careful," Beth said, pointing to my hand. It shook as I brought my coffee cup to my lips. "You're going to spill it all over you."

"He shouldn't be affecting me like this." I didn't like it.

She patted my back. "Remember you have a fine-ass man and don't need him."

"Doesn't need who?" The deep voice sent chills down my arms. He stepped into the room, wearing a sexy grin on his face.

If he thought I was going to answer him, he was wrong. I decided to pretend he wasn't there. That's how mature women handled such situations.

Beth snorted as she watched our interaction.

He moved his head to the side and took the seat right next to me.

"I'm surprised Lover Boy isn't hovering over you." He waved his hand toward my bag. "I mean, Lord forbid you have to carry your own things to class."

He used to do this shit when we were younger. He'd say something to piss me off, usually about my pack and acting out. He'd do this when he was having some sort of family problems. I'd always thought it was because he felt safe with me. What a fucking joke.

I kept my eyes forward and ignored the buzzing of my skin.

"You should take the hint." Beth shook her head as she glanced from him to me.

"I'm thinking you should butt out." He didn't even bother acknowledging her. His eyes stayed on me. "Or can Angel not fight her own battles?"

That was the nickname he'd started calling me right around the time my feelings for him had begun to change. He'd said I was too sweet to be from this realm. It hurt so damn much to hear it again. But he wanted a reaction, and he was used to getting what he wanted.

"Aw, I guess she can't." He let out a dark laugh. "Why am I not surprised?"

"You've really become one huge son of a bitch." The sweet boy from my memories wasn't here anymore. "But what else could I expect from a Murphy."

"How typical of you to bring up my pack." He crossed his arms over his chest. "You guys are the abominations."

Beth snorted. "You weren't kidding about your packs being rivals."

"Ahh, she was talking about me?" A huge smirk filled his face.

It wasn't a question. It was a statement. The arrogant ass. "It wasn't about you. Just about back home."

"So naturally, my pack would come up." He arched an eyebrow. "Bullshit."

When had he become such an asshole? "Believe what you want. I don't care."

"You sure about that?" He leaned toward me, and his scent grew stronger. "Did you get my text yesterday?" He leaned even closer, invading my senses.

My body responded to him, and I hated it. He knew he still influenced me.

Students filled the classroom, oblivious to our conversation.

"Why don't you leave her alone?" Beth's voice took on an edge as she side-eyed him. "It's obvious she's not interested."

I appreciated her helping me out, but I already knew what his response would be.

"That's not what her smell is telling me," he said low, barely loud enough for me to hear, but the words also seemed to scream at me.

The professor came into the class and blissfully started the lecture.

I DIDN'T bother rushing from class to Precalculus. I picked up my backpack and slung it over my shoulder.

Beth stood beside me, and the two of us headed toward the door.

"Will you be okay?" she asked, looking worried.

I hated it. She hadn't known me for long, and she was already concerned. I was that friend: the one who didn't have her shit together so others felt obligated to care. "Yeah, I'm fine."

As soon as we hit the first floor, Beth waved and headed to her class in the other building.

Aidan

All class, I felt like I was bipolar. One minute, I wanted to be friendly, and the next, I wanted to strike out in anger. Both emotions were driven by my need to be with her. It was a lose-lose situation. Either way, we just kept hurting each other.

I had to accept that she wouldn't be in my life long term. Our being together wouldn't work anyway. She deserved a full life and a chance to be happy even if it wasn't with me, which just pissed me off all over again.

This was my last chance to learn what she'd been up to these past four years.

Emma

"Emma," Aidan called out, but I pressed on.

I hurried into the classroom and sat in the same seat as yesterday.

"You do realize I have the same class." He slid into the seat next to mine. "How are things?"

"Really?" I asked. He acted like we were old friends.

"Yeah, it's been a while." He shrugged and winced a little. "I figured you'd have a long-ass story to tell me, like old times."

If humans hadn't been in the room with us, I would have slapped him across the face. He had some nerve. "Yeah, someone who suddenly disappeared in my life has popped back up and is acting like nothing strange ever happened." I was tired of people pushing me around.

He coughed and nodded. "I deserved that." He ran his hands through his hair. "You're not as big of a pushover..."

"Any longer?" So that's how he viewed me. Good to know.

"Sure... we'll go with that." He blew out a breath.

I faced the front of the class and stiffened. "Thanks for..." There wasn't a good way to end this sentence. "...nothing."

He leaned back in his seat and pulled out his book.

"I don't think I've ever seen you as happy as after these past two Dance classes." Jacob was once again standing outside my locker room, waiting on me.

"Yeah, they've been great." I walked over and smiled. "It's fun again. When I was involved in all of that cheerleading stuff, it was so stringent and focused more on cheering than dance. That's why I wanted to go back to what made me the happiest."

He took my bag from me and then grabbed my hand. "I'll be honest. I thought you were making a horrible decision, but not anymore. You were right."

"So I do know a thing or two." I followed his lead as we started heading toward the science building. That one word already dampened my happiness. I had to stop. I was letting one boy influence me too much.

"I can't wait until we're done with this lab." Jacob frowned. "Maybe I can talk to the professor and see if he'll force that guy to switch."

"It's not worth it." I decided to pretend Aidan was no one. It shouldn't be that hard.

"You seem eager to drop it." Jacob's voice turned the cold tone that he only reserved for others. He'd never talked to me like that before.

"He's messing with us. The more we react, the more he'll enjoy it."

"You're right." He huffed and gently squeezed my hand. "I'm sorry. I'm being a dick, but it'd help if you were more loving toward me in front of him."

Of course, that's where he'd go with this. "He's doing it on purpose. Let's not let him get to us."

We hurried to class, and Jacob headed to my chair to drop off my bag. As usual, Aidan was already there.

"Is she injured?" Aidan flicked his finger at the bag.

"No. She can carry it herself, but I like taking care of her." Jacob turned to me and brushed his lips against mine. "One day, you might understand."

"Probably not. My girl would be able to stand on her own two feet." Aidan lifted a hand. "To each their own."

Jacob linked me as he glared at Aidan. *We need to switch seats.*

No, it's fine. I touched his arm. *I promise.*

You'll let me know? Jacob kissed my forehead.

Promise.

When I sat down next to him and Jacob headed over to his seat, Aidan shifted his body in my direction. "I thought Lover Boy was gonna try to switch with me again."

"Nope, he's not threatened by you." My skin buzzed uncomfortably from our proximity.

"Well, then he's a dumbass." He scooted closer, and our arms brushed.

The shock of it jolted me to the core, and he jumped back, eyes widening.

No... it couldn't be. He was my fated. That's why I couldn't get over him.

"Why now?" I turned to him, needing an answer.

His face was a mask of indifference. "What are you

talking about?"

"What are you trying to do?" I wanted to see if he'd tell me the truth.

"I... I don't know." His shoulders tensed, and he turned his gaze to the whiteboard. "I didn't mean for this to happen. This was a huge mistake."

The words cut me. "Of course, it is. Why didn't you show up that night?"

The wince told me everything. "I... I can't and won't tell you that."

"Then we have nothing left to say." I turned my attention to the front of the class and pulled out my books.

"Emma..."

"Yeah?" I stared into his eyes.

"I really am sorry." His shoulders sagged, and pain similar to mine filled his face.

"Don't." I lifted a hand and pointed at him. "Don't you dare. We can't be friends—hell, not even acquaintances, so leave me the hell alone." I let the anger consume me. I needed it to get through this.

Aidan

HER ANGER toward me was a good thing. I had to keep repeating those words. But damn, she looked so hurt. I wished I could tell her why I'd left, but the whole reason I'd disappeared was so she'd never have to worry or deal with my burden.

I'd done it because I'd loved her. I still did. But it was more important to see her alive, even if she wasn't mine, than to live in a world without her.

CHAPTER SEVEN

Emma

The next several weeks passed in a blur. I was determined not to interact with Aidan any more than necessary, and he obviously felt the same way.

It still tormented me to be so close to him, but I would simply learn how to deal with it. I wasn't sure if it was worse not seeing him or seeing him every day. For the longest time, I'd hoped and prayed for a glimpse of him, but I'd learned to be careful what I asked for.

The homecoming game was this evening, and Beth and I were in our room getting ready. The game started at six, but we wanted to get there earlier to enjoy the tailgating aspect of it.

"Who are we even going to hang out with?" Beyond Jacob and his football friends, we hadn't really socialized with anyone else.

"We'll figure it out." She combed my hair. "Worst case, we end up in a bar and sweet-talk the bartender into letting us drink."

"I think there will be plenty of drinking tonight after the game." One of the juniors on the team was holding a party at a house he and a few other players rented. Jacob had insisted we go.

"Yeah, but we're wolves." She used a curling iron to add waves to my hair. "We have to start early. You know that."

It was harder for wolves to get drunk than it was for humans. It was a blessing and a curse. It meant knocking back drinks, and if you didn't want to sober up, you had to keep up the same pace all night.

I hated not being in control, so I never allowed myself to drink like that. When you drank, your tongue got loose. I'd had to take care of Jacob, Libby, and Grace most of the time anyway.

Beth picked up a section of my hair by my left ear. "I didn't know you had a tattoo." She touched my birthmark. "What does the star represent?"

"Believe it or not, it's a birthmark," I answered as she worked on that section of hair.

"Well, that's pretty damn cool." She ran the curling iron through my hair. "It's like perfect formation. You totally could play it off as a tattoo."

"You know, I can do my hair just fine." To be honest, I was a little worried. She'd insisted on doing my hair and makeup, and even though her makeup looked great, she wore it much darker than me.

"Nope, I'm doing it." She picked up hairspray and lightly sprayed it all over my hair. "Now it's makeup time." She took in my Crawford University football jersey. It contained their mascot—a howling black wolf—with a royal blue background and had Jacob's last name and number on the back. "So, we're going with the devoted college girl look?" She waved her hand up and down in front of me.

"I have to wear it." He had been so happy when he'd given me the jersey. He'd had it made for me, and he'd even told my parents about it. "He'd be hurt if I didn't."

"Now, you know I think Jacob is one of the nicest guys I've ever met, but it's almost like he's trying to mark his territory and he's manipulating you. He's always playing the *oh, but I love you* card." She adjusted her see-through jersey with a black sports bra underneath. It left little to the imagination when paired with her black skirt and combat boots. Somehow, she rocked the look. "It's gotten worse since a certain someone hasn't been able to take his eyes off you."

"What?" That had to be an exaggeration. Ever since that day in Chemistry when he'd acted like an ass, we'd barely talked. He grunted and groaned more than anything. "We've barely said more than a few words to each other. Chemistry class has been interesting. He points more to the book than speaks."

"That may be true, but in English, he stares at you the entire time." Beth grabbed some makeup brushes off her table and told me to turn around on the bed.

I looked at her color palette of dark grays and blues. I opened my mouth to say something, but she held up her hand.

"Nope, I'm doing this." She grabbed my foundation powder. "If you hate it, you can take it off and do it yourself."

I couldn't argue. "Fine." The win was we'd get out of here later if I had to redo my makeup. Tailgating wasn't my idea of fun.

She went to town on my face, her hands moving fast and efficiently. "Jacob has noticed how much attention he pays to you."

"Nah, he's thrilled that Aidan and I are barely speaking." He wasn't anxious anymore when we headed to class, and even though I was still torn up about Aidan, I'd never felt happier. I knew I'd missed dance, but I hadn't realized how much. That was a piece of me that was tied to no one else.

"Because he was afraid you were interested in him. Close your eyes." She dabbed something on my eyelids. "Now that you guys aren't talking, he isn't freaking out, but he's concerned."

"It'll be fine." Her fingertips were like cool sponges on my skin. I hadn't had someone do my makeup in such a long time that it was kind of weird. "Aidan and I aren't a thing." I hadn't told her that he was my fated yet. I was afraid it would make it more real.

"Not yet, at least," she mumbled, and I didn't feel like correcting her, which was a problem in itself.

"Okay, I'm done." She set her brush on her small table. "Here, look." She handed me the mirror, and what I saw surprised me.

She'd made my eyes a smoky blue that wasn't overbearing but darker than my usual makeup. My gray eyes seemed lighter and slightly blue.

My lips were painted a nude pink that was only a few shades darker than my natural color. This was probably the best makeup I'd ever had done.

I glanced at her and smiled. "You did amazing."

"Yes, I did." She took the mirror and held it back so I could see my hair. "I told you I work magic." She snickered.

"That, you do." My friendship with her had gotten to be so natural it was scary. I hadn't felt this close to anyone outside of... We didn't need to go there.

She examined her face in the mirror. Her makeup was

her typical layered look, but she had blood-red lips this time. "Let's go," she said and headed to the door.

We were soon walking across the campus toward the football stadium. A large group of students was hanging around the parking lot, and people were sitting on tailgates.

"Hey, Beth." A guy with short brown hair stumbled over to us. He scanned her from head to toe, and then his eyes narrowed on me. "And Beth's super-hot friend," he slurred and swayed.

"Someone's had a little too much to drink." Beth took the beer from his hands and poured it out.

"What the hell?" The guy started and looked from his beer being poured to Beth. "That's not cool."

"What's not cool is you leering at us." She handed the empty can back to him. "Our eyes are up here," she said, pointing to her face.

I had to admit she had a point. I wasn't even wearing anything low cut, and it was obvious where he had been looking.

Another guy came over and took his friend by the arm. "Come on, man. You need water so you don't pass out during the game."

"Nah, I'm fine." The guy stumbled off back to his friends.

"Sorry about that," the new guy said. He looked a few years older than us, and an earthy scent filled the air. He leaned toward us, his sage eyes sparkling. His hair was chestnut brown and down to his shoulders. His face was smooth, and his lips tilted upward. "You know how humans can be."

He was a witch. Even though books claimed that only women were witches, it wasn't true. A witch could be male, female, or anything in between.

"Indeed." Beth turned her head toward me and crossed her arms. "Then, why are you here?"

He smiled. "To experience college—just like you." He motioned for us to follow him, and we made our way to a group of three hanging around a truck spaced apart from the rest of the people. "First off, my name is Samuel," he said and turned to the group. "And these are my friends."

"Hi, my name is Amethyst." The girl jumped off the bed of the truck and extended her hand to us. Her eyes were purple, which must have been where she'd gotten her name. Her long, dirty blonde hair was pulled into a low ponytail, and I had at least two inches on her.

Unsure what else to do, I shook her hand. Wolves and witches didn't hate one another. Some packs even took them in. The alliance was mutually beneficial. We protected them from the outside world, and they healed and tended to the sick. At one point, our pack had had a witch living among us, but she'd vanished several years before I was born.

"Oh." Her eyes widened. "I didn't realize you held magic."

Okay, that was strange. "I'm a wolf," I said low enough so humans couldn't hear but loud enough so they could.

Her brows furrowed. "You're not a witch?"

"No." She had to have lost her damn mind.

"Just ignore her." The girl beside her leaned forward to see me. Her red hair fell to the side, and her crystal blue eyes shone. "She's learning how to read energy. Her grandmother could, and it's a lost art to our kind."

"Yeah." Amethyst frowned. "But I'm determined to get

there. She left her diary on how she learned to control her power."

"I'm Coral, by the way." The redhead saluted us.

"And I'm Finn." The guy was around my height, and his eyes were amber. It was unsettling how wolf-like he seemed. His auburn hair made him look even more off-kilter. He was slender, but there was something hard inside him. "So, now that we've told you all our secrets, it's your turn."

"Nothing special about us." I shrugged. "I'm Emma."

"Speak for yourself." Beth lifted her chin. "And I'm Beth. We're both freshmen."

"That's why we haven't seen you before." Samuel nodded. "I'm glad you aren't part of a pack that has a problem with us." He rolled his eyes. "Our first year here, we ran into one of your kind that wasn't very accepting."

"What happened?" I didn't understand packs like that. Some of them were so antiquated in their ways. Our species needed to evolve to become better and stronger and survive.

"It was fine." Finn sighed dramatically. "We had one little altercation, and when we showed him what we could do, the pup ran away. He avoided us the rest of his time here."

"So, you ladies going to the game?" Coral nodded toward the stadium. "We were going to head in there soon. Maybe we can sit together."

"It's really nice being around other supernaturals." Amethyst smiled. "We've always believed we should be one with shifters. You guys are half-humans, after all."

"Well, princess here has special seats." Beth pointed at me.

Hey, babe? I doubted there was anything he could do, but it didn't hurt to ask.

You here? he answered immediately.

Yeah, we're about to come in. Do you think I could get four more people in our section?

Four more people? There was something in his tone that I'd never heard before. *Who are they?*

Some witches who go here. I wasn't sure how he would respond. *Beth wanted to come out to the tailgate area, and we made some new friends.*

Oh, yeah. He sounded relieved. *Just tell the ushers they're with you. It'll be fine. Let me know when you get here so I can see you in that jersey. I'm glad Prescott's mom made some for us. I won't lie, though. I wish you were still on the sidelines.*

He kept pushing the issue, and it was starting to piss me off. *Nope, sorry. If it's that important to you, then we're going to have a problem.*

No, it's fine. Sounding a little regretful, he turned on the waterworks. *I just liked you being there and close by. That's all.*

I'm not that much farther away. Beth and I had been to every game, and the cheerleaders were right in front of us most of the time. *You'll be fine.*

"He said it should be fine if you sit with us." We didn't have assigned seats per se, but we were at the front of the student section. The stadium staff knew who to let inside at the very front.

"Sweet. I wished witches could mind link like pack wolves," Amethyst said. "But it's still cool to watch. Let's go."

We headed through the students who were packing up to move into the stadium. When the six of us got in line, an uneasy feeling once again coursed down my back. I turned around but didn't see anything out of the ordinary.

"What's wrong?" Beth glanced at me from the corner of her eye.

"Just feel like we're being watched." I had to stop being paranoid. Lately, I'd been getting this feeling pretty often. Well, ever since I'd gotten to the university.

She scanned the area. "I don't see anything."

"Yeah, I'm probably imagining things." I decided to brush it off.

Inside the stadium, the six of us headed down to our normal section right at the bottom. The usher turned and nodded without checking my ticket.

I pointed to the group behind me. "They're with me."

"Not a problem." He moved to let us all through the small gate.

"Wow. This is amazing." Amethyst scanned our seats. "How did you get these seats?"

Beth snorted and shook her head. "The jersey doesn't tell you that loud and clear?"

"Wait... Rogers?" Finn's eyes went straight to the field where the football team was warming up. "The quarterback?"

"Yeah, he's my..." The word still didn't feel natural on my lips. "... boyfriend."

"I told you he was one of them." Finn stuck his finger in Samuel's direction.

"Fine, you win." Samuel went over and sat in a chair that put him close to midfield.

It was almost as if Jacob had heard us talking about him because he turned toward us and waved.

I waved back, feeling like an idiot, but I knew I should be nice.

Coral sat next to Samuel and asked, "So how long have you two been dating?"

"Over two years." I didn't want to talk about our relationship right now, especially when that uneasy feeling hadn't gone away. "I'm going to go grab a Coke before the game starts. Do you all need anything?"

"Nope, I'm good." Amethyst smiled while the other three shook their heads.

"Mind getting me a drink too?" Beth asked as she sat next to Coral. She knew I was trying to get away from the conversation.

"Will do." I headed back up the stairs to the concession stands. At the top, my skin began to buzz.

Aidan

LIKE A CREEPER, I couldn't stay away, and now I was pissed.

I stood at the gate, watching Emma talk with her new witchy friends. What was the point of leaving her if she was going to wind up as a target anyway?

To make matters worse, she looked hot as sin and was wearing that idiot douchebag's jersey. I'd never felt so damn hurt or angry before.

She walked past the others and headed up the stairs. She was being pulled in my direction, which made this whole idiotic dance we were doing even worse.

I had to get through to her.

Emma

Suddenly, a hand yanked me into a strong chest.

Every part of my body was on fire.

"Dammit." Aidan released me and stumbled several feet back, putting distance between us.

Even with the space between us, his eyes went to my lips.

Without thinking, I stepped into him, and his head lowered as if he might kiss me.

Even though I was desperate to feel his lips, I couldn't do it, not after the way he'd been treating me and not while I was with Jacob.

Right before his lips could touch mine, I stepped back. Instead, I focused on the fact that he was being an ass. "What the hell are you doing?" He hadn't talked to me in weeks, and now he'd grabbed me. That's not how this worked.

"No, it's me who should be asking that question." His nostrils flared as he eyed the group I'd just left.

"What are you talking about?"

"Why are you hanging out with witches?" He asked quietly, and his breathing increased.

"We just met them." Wait, I didn't need to explain a damn thing to him. "And it's none of your business."

"Like hell, it's not." He took one step toward me and stopped. "You don't need to be around those crazies."

"Oh, that's right." How had I forgotten? "Your pack hates them. Well, mine doesn't. And they're nice. Who I hang out with is none of your concern." I turned around to go get the drinks. "So fuck off."

"Do you think you get to walk away from me?" He nearly growled.

I spun around and glared at him. I hoped he felt how much I hated him. "Well, I did learn from the best."

Something crossed his face, but it was so quick I wasn't sure what. "Fine." He began to turn away but paused. "By the way, that jersey looks like shit on you."

Asshole. "Thanks. I'll make sure to wear it more often." I forced my feet to move forward and leave him behind. Maybe he'd finally feel a fraction of the hurt he'd caused me.

CHAPTER EIGHT

The usher allowed me inside, and as I walked back to the witches and Beth, I forced a smile on my face. I must have been more distracted that I realized and came down the wrong row since Finn now sat beside Samuel closest to midfield. So I continued past them, Coral, and Beth to sit on the other side of Amethyst.

I reached over Amethyst and handed the second drink to Beth. "Here you go."

"Thanks," she said as she scanned me. "You okay?"

"Yeah." I would be. I needed to get him out of my mind, though. It didn't help that the creepy, funny feeling remained. It was obvious it had to do with Aidan. Why was he watching me so damn much? For someone who'd made a point to avoid me, he sure had picked up some creepy hobbies.

"She's lying." Amethyst crossed her legs. "There is so much negative energy coming off her."

"Yeah, I know. Did you run into you know who?" Beth asked.

She and I had gotten so close that I couldn't lie to her again. "Yeah, but it's fine."

"Oh... is it a boy?" Amethyst's eyes glowed.

"Of course it is." Coral giggled. "And I'm assuming it's not the boyfriend, seeing as he's trying to get her attention right now on the field."

Are you okay? Jacob's voice in my mind almost startled me.

I looked down to find him standing in front of me.

The platform was five feet off the ground, but with him being over six feet, he could reach me. He raised his arms and placed his hands around my ankles.

"Yeah, I'm fine. The line was crazy, and for a second, I didn't think I'd get down here before the game started." That wasn't a lie. The line had taken ten minutes to go through, but I'd conveniently left out the Aidan part.

"No worries. You made it." He looked at the others. "Those your new friends?"

"Yeah. I figured you'd meet them after the game."

"Sounds perfect." He smiled.

"Rogers, get your ass over here. It's time for us to go in," the coach yelled at him.

I nodded at him. "You better go."

"Yeah." He pouted. "Kiss for good luck?"

"You know I can't do that." I batted his hand away.

"Rain check then." He winked at me.

"The coach is watching." I forced a giggle. "Now go on."

"Fine." He fake pouted again for a second before he ran off to join the rest of the team.

Beth shook her head. "Between the jersey and the kiss, that was him peeing all over you."

"I love it when shifters make dog jokes." Samuel lifted a fist in the air. "It makes my day."

"Yeah, but you're not allowed to." Beth narrowed her eyes at him. "Only we can do it."

"See, where's the fun in that?" He sighed as if she'd just ruined his day.

"Oh, stop it." Coral smacked him on the arm.

"Aw." He grabbed his arm, pretending she'd hurt him. "Wait until I tell the Priestess what you did."

"Yeah, let me be there when you tell her." Coral snickered. "I don't want to miss her reaction."

"Are you all from the same coven?" I hadn't even considered that they would be. I'd figured they'd met each other by chance.

"Yeah." Amethyst pointed to the other three. "We are. We all grew up together."

"That's neat." Libby and Grace had always known they'd stay home and close to the pack. I'd always known I'd be going to school alone. Or at least, I'd thought I would be.

"You guys aren't from the same pack?" Finn glanced at me and then to Beth. "You two seem awfully close."

"Yeah, we get along." Beth grinned at me. "Back home, I never really felt like I fit in, so it's refreshing to have found a good friend."

She'd never told me that before. She never really talked about anyone back home, except for her parents and older brother. And even then, I'd needed to connect the dots.

"Hey, I kinda feel the same way." I was the orphan. Even though my parents treated me like their blood, I'd always felt like an outsider. Something felt different inside me. That was one reason why it had hurt so damn hard when Aidan had ghosted me. He was the only one who'd really seen me. All of me. It was nice now to have the same feeling with Beth.

The crowd cheered as the football team ran onto the field.

I'd been so caught up in the conversation that I hadn't even noticed it was time. I jumped to my feet and cheered. After all, that was what he wanted me to do.

Aidan

OF COURSE, the gorgeous, stubborn-ass wouldn't listen to me. Not only was she hanging out with the very people who could get her killed, but she was cheering for her asshole football boyfriend.

I'd never felt jealous of anything in my entire life, but she brought it out in me. Even my older brother, as the alpha heir, didn't faze me.

My legs propelled me forward, and I didn't even try to stop. I was making a huge mistake, but I didn't give a fuck. Protecting her was more important than anything else.

Emma

SOON THE GAME BEGAN. Right when I was about to sit down again, the buzzing of my skin picked up, and I heard an all too familiar voice. "I'm with them."

"She didn't say you were." The usher stood tall, but his hands shook.

Aidan was a strong wolf, and even humans could feel the power.

"He's not." What the hell was he trying to pull?

"Oh, who's that?" Amethyst's focused on Aidan.

"Either let me in or I'll make you." Aidan shrugged. "Up to you."

"Fine, but only this one time." The usher's bottom lip quivered.

"What? No." I stood and stalked over to the douchebag. "Go away. You're not wanted."

"Aw, I think someone is protesting a little too much." He slid past the usher, and then his eyes turned dark, nearly brown, as he took in the four witches. "What do we have here?"

Finn stood and stared Aidan down. "You have a problem?" He pulled out a knife from his pocket, moving so no one but us could see.

"Yeah, you shouldn't be hanging around her." Aidan seemed unfazed and pointed at me.

"Dammit, Finn. Put that away." Coral lifted an eyebrow as she took in the shifter. "Who are you?"

"It's none of your damn business, shrew." Aidan's nose wrinkled in disgust. "Shouldn't you be sticking to your own kind?"

Samuel stood, refusing to be looked down upon. "Who the fuck do you think you are?"

Holy shit. This wouldn't end well.

What is going on, Emma? Jacob's voice was low and angry.

I... I don't know. Not only was Aidan causing problems with my new friends, but he was causing problems with Jacob, too. Great. I made my way back to my seat to put distance between Aidan and me.

"Emma said you weren't welcome, mutt." Finn sneered as he put the knife back in his pocket, but his hand stayed there. "So why are you still here?"

"Emma doesn't know what she wants," Aidan warned. "It's best if you stay out of our business."

We had the full attention of everyone near us. "Aidan, just stop, okay."

"If you're going to stay, sit down." Beth met his gaze head-on. "You're causing a scene."

"Fine." Aidan walked past the rest of them and sat right next to me.

"What do you think you're doing?" I wanted to punch his face.

"Watching a football game," he grumbled as he crossed his arms and focused on the field.

"You're causing problems." He acted as if he wanted to make me miserable.

"Good." He refused to look at me. "You shouldn't be hanging around people like them." His eyes glanced at the witch beside me.

"What have we ever done to you?" Amethyst huffed. "Packs like yours give wolves a bad name."

"Your existence is problematic," Aidan growled low. "Your kind shouldn't even exist."

"Then yours shouldn't either," Coral hissed.

Why is he sitting next to you? Jacob's voice was devoid of emotion.

I'd never heard him talk like that before. *I don't know.*

Did you tell the usher he was with you? Jacob was on the field, getting ready for a play.

No, I didn't. If he didn't concentrate, he would mess up. *He threatened the usher. You need to pay attention to your game.*

How the hell am I supposed to do that when my girl is sitting beside another guy?

"Can you please just go away?" I couldn't believe I just said those words to him.

"Wow, I'm getting mixed signals. First, you demand to know why I left, and now you're telling me to go." He rolled his eyes and focused forward. "But you're a woman, so what should I have expected?"

He was an asshole. Anger, instead of hurt, fueled me, and I welcomed the change. Hate I could focus and lash out with. "It must be lonely."

"What the fuck does that mean?" His body went rigid like I'd hit a nerve.

"You're miserable." That much was clear. It surprised me that it'd taken me this long to see it. "You spew hate at everyone else, and I'm done being your punching bag."

"So, you've got it all figured out?" His penetrating gaze glued me to my spot.

"No, but I'm learning to be okay with it." He'd been the center of my focus for so long that I'd forgotten who I was. Hell, I'd never figured it out, to begin with.

He moved quickly, touching my hand. The buzzing was like electricity shooting between us. My traitorous body reacted, and I nearly let out a moan.

My eyes locked on his, and something passed between us as though we were both acknowledging what we were to each other.

"Oh, shit." Beth jumped to her feet, and she grabbed my arm.

"What?" I pulled my eyes away from him and followed Beth's gaze.

The referees were pulling football players off a pile.

"We need a stretcher," a ref called. "Now."

Jacob was at the bottom, and he wasn't moving at all.

The coach ran out to the field. Everything clicked at that moment. Jacob was hurt, and it was my fault.

Jacob? I tried our mental link, but it was radio silence on the other side.

"Emma." Beth was at my side, grabbing my arm. Her mouth moved, but I couldn't hear a damn thing.

"What?" I closed my eyes and shook my head.

"We've got to go." Though Beth's words had broken through, I couldn't comprehend them.

Aidan pulled me to his chest.

The fire shot through my skin, breaking me from my daze. "Hey, Angel," he said softly, reminding me of the boy I used to know.

No. I wasn't sure if I spoke the words or said them in my head, but I yanked from his grasp and shook my head. "You've done enough."

"Let's get you out of here." He lifted his hands in the air as if that made him safe.

"I'm not going anywhere with you." Even though I wanted to blame him for what had gone down with Jacob, I couldn't. This was on me. I'd been weak enough to allow Aidan to exist in my life. I hadn't shut him down because, apparently, I enjoyed the pain.

"I'll help you get to him," Samuel said as he stood, and right when he was about to head toward the stairs, Aidan grabbed his shoulder, snapping him away from me.

"She's staying with me." Aidan's voice quavered with rage.

"Yes. Yes, that's a good idea," I growled and pushed both hands into Aidan's chest, forcing him backward. "I'm done with whatever this is between us."

"You're done?" Aidan's eyebrows lifted, and I wasn't

sure if he was surprised by my words or that I was strong enough to make him move.

"This isn't healthy." But neither was my relationship with Jacob. I was being unfair toward him and myself.

Right now, I had to make sure Jacob was okay. That was my priority. "I'd really appreciate it if you took me," I said to Samuel.

"Of course." He headed toward the stairs again.

"I'll go with you." Beth took my hand and pulled me to follow after the witches.

"Emma." Aidan pleaded.

I wasn't sure what he expected from me. He'd been trying to control me tonight, and that wasn't okay. He'd insulted my new friends, upset my boyfriend, and was purposely fucking with my mind. I followed Beth, not even bothering to glance over my shoulder.

Aidan

IT HURT WATCHING her walk away after the way we'd connected. That's probably how she'd felt all those years ago.

I'd fucked it up so much, and I wasn't sure if I could fix it. Dammit, she was my fated mate. There was no denying it. I needed her, but we couldn't be together. My family wouldn't allow me to claim someone marked.

It wasn't a simple decision: her or them. It was a lot more complicated than that. But each time I saw her, it got more difficult to remember why I was fighting our bond so hard in the first place.

Emma

Luckily, the staff didn't give me trouble as I made my way down to the locker room. I knocked on the door, and when the coach opened it, he waved me in.

Beth smiled. "We'll stay out here and wait for you."

I ran into the room. "Jacob?"

"Emma." His speech was slurred, but he was talking.

I ran over to him and pulled him into a huge hug. "Are you okay?"

"He's got a good concussion." The trainer pursed his lips and nodded. "But he's recovering well."

"I need to get back out there." Jacob stood and almost fell.

If I hadn't been next to him, he would've hit the ground hard.

"No, no playing for you." The trainer patted Jacob's shoulder. "You need to get to your dorm and rest."

"I can take him." I wrapped my arm around his waist, allowing him to put some of his weight on me.

"You'll need some help." The coach opened the door and paused when he saw the five people waiting on us. "Well, it looks like you have plenty."

"Yeah." For once, I felt lucky to have some actual friends in my corner. "Finn or Samuel, do you mind?"

"Sure." Finn wrapped Jacob's arm around his shoulders. "Let's go get him settled."

"He needs to eat and stay awake for a few hours." The coach walked behind us. "He'll have a pounding headache for a while too. If you have trouble waking him, call us immediately. My number is in his phone."

"Got it. Thanks."

The seven of us walked slowly through the stadium and out the back door.

"How did humans hurt you so badly?" Samuel asked once we were away from prying ears.

"The two who got to me first are wolves." He shook his head and sighed. "I lost track of them, and they got me."

He'd been too worried about Aidan sitting next to me that he'd lost focus.

"Why don't you come stay with us tonight?" Amethyst asked as we walked into the parking lot. "We have a house just a few blocks from campus. You can stay in the living room."

That was probably the best idea. I couldn't stay with him at his dorm, and we could get in trouble if he stayed in ours. "Are you sure?" Normally, I didn't trust people right away, but for some reason, I felt okay with them. "It would be easier to keep an eye on him."

"Sure." Coral smiled. "The more the merrier."

"Are you okay with that?" I didn't want Jacob to be uncomfortable with the arrangement.

"Yeah, it's fine." He grimaced with pain. "I just need to grab a change of clothes first."

"So do I." And I wanted to wash my makeup off too.

"Here." Samuel took my spot under Jacob's other arm. "You go ahead and grab your stuff, and we'll drive him to his dorm and meet you girls at the house."

"Let's go." Coral pulled the keys out of her small pocket and jangled them.

Beth's brows furrowed. "You guys drove separately?"

"Yeah, he's got that truck." She pointed to the one they'd been sitting in when we'd met them. "And we need more space." She headed to a newer Honda Civic.

The four of us climbed in, and soon, we were outside the dorms. When I climbed out of the car, the nagging feeling ran down my spine again.

I turned around, expecting not to find Aidan, but he was across the street, leaning against a tree. Our eyes connected, and he motioned for me to come to him.

Yeah, that wasn't happening. I turned around and walked directly into the dorm. Some things were meant to stay broken.

CHAPTER NINE

As soon as Beth and I entered our dorm room, she spun to face me. "What the hell was that back there?"

"Which part?" I would rather answer her question directly instead of pouring my heart and soul out.

"Aidan." Her word was simple, but so much was packed behind it.

"Look, I don't know." I walked over, grabbed one of my bags, and started packing my clothes. "His pack hates witches."

"So, he just showed up to make an ass of himself?" She put a pair of pajamas in my bag. "You don't mind if I share with you?"

"Yeah, you can, but don't feel obligated to come." I felt awful, inconveniencing everyone, but I owed it to Jacob to take care of him.

"Yes, I do." Beth snorted. "How did Aidan know you were hanging around witches?"

"I don't know. You know how I felt like someone was watching me?"

She nodded.

"It was Aidan." I steadied myself for what came next. "When I went to get our drinks, he grabbed me..." And pulled me into his arms before getting away from me as fast as possible. However, I didn't want to share those details.

"And?" She sat on her bed.

"He told me not to hang around them and that my jersey looked like shit on me." I threw my hairbrush into the bag with an extra change of clothes.

"The last part is because he's jealous of Jacob." She went to the closet and started going through her clothes.

"Well, that's too bad." He was acting like he was the victim, not me. "He left me. He can go to hell."

"I agree." She put her outfit in the bag and lifted her hands. "He was a complete asshole to our new friends."

"He's been an asshole to everyone." None of it even made sense. "It's hard to believe he's the same boy I knew."

"It sounds like his pack is awful, but hell, so is mine." She lifted a hand. "My pack isn't fond of witches either."

"You don't seem to have a problem with them." It was strange. How many packs hated them? Were her and Aidan's packs different, or was it mine?

"Because I believe every person should be given the benefit of the doubt." She glanced out the window. "Their race shouldn't define them. Those four seem nice, and until they prove me wrong, I'm down with being their friend. But that doesn't mean I'm leaving you alone in their house overnight."

"Jacob will be there." I hated that she felt obligated to go.

"You mean the guy with a huge concussion." She waggled her brows.

"We both know he'll be better by morning." Wolves

healed extremely fast. What took a human a week to heal only took us a day or two. That's why going to a hospital was a huge no-no.

"But probably not tonight." She waved toward the door. "Come on, let's go. We can get settled in before the guys get there."

That was probably a good idea. "All right."

"Here we are." Coral pulled into the driveway of an older two-story house right past the edge of campus. "Home sweet home."

The truck was missing, so we'd beat the guys here. That made sense seeing as the guys were helping Jacob get his things together. It was probably slow going.

Amethyst opened her door and gestured for us to follow her. "Let's get everything situated."

As we stood from the car, I realized it was only about eight in the evening. The football game was still going on. "I'm sorry if we ruined your plans tonight." I hadn't even thought about it until now.

"No, you're good." Coral headed to the front door and put the key into the lock. "We're headed back home tomorrow, so we wouldn't be going to parties anyway. Inevitably, Finn would have gotten drunk and begun telling all his secrets.

Beth followed behind me. "He doesn't seem like the secret type. He's more like the reserved and suffer-in-silence type."

"Oh, he is." Coral laughed as she opened the door. "Unless he's drunk. So you've been warned."

"Then, he refuses to get up in the morning because he

needs to sleep it off." Amethyst swayed from side to side. "So in a way, you've done us a favor."

"How far away is your coven?" I asked as I stepped into the house.

We entered straight into the living room. The ceilings were about seven feet high, and the walls were all white. It had maple floors with a plaid couch sitting in front of an old brick fireplace. There were two matching love seats on each side and a television mounted over the fireplace. A large staircase right in front of the door led to the second floor.

"Two hours south of Atlanta." Amethyst smiled. "It's in a small town you've probably never heard of."

Across the living room, a doorway revealed a table.

"So the kitchen is through the door on the left, and the downstairs bathroom is underneath the stairs." Coral pointed to a door I hadn't noticed yet.

When she'd said "underneath the stairs," she hadn't been lying.

"So, who the hell was that jackass who forced his way into our section?" Coral sat on the large couch on one side.

That was a fair question, and one I wasn't sure how to answer. "Someone I knew several years ago. His pack hates witches for some reason, and they hate our pack for not having a problem with your kind."

"So it's a Romeo and Juliet type thing." Amethyst sat on the same couch but on the other side. "But he still has a lot to understand about himself first."

"I'm not sure that's a good comparison." We didn't need anyone romanticizing our dysfunctional relationship.

"Fate always makes sure her choices pan out." Amethyst tried comforting me.

How the hell did she know? Yes, we were fated mates,

and our bond was there. But we weren't sealing it. There was no way in hell, even if I wanted to. I wouldn't be controlled or cower. He'd left me for God knew what reason.

"Fate?" Beth paused and focused on me. "Have you been withholding information?"

The guys could arrive at any second. This was not a conversation I needed them to walk in on. But she'd know if I lied, so I stayed silent.

"Emma Hart!" Beth sucked in some air, and her eyes darkened. "He's your fated mate, and you didn't tell me."

"It changes nothing." The truth rang so loudly with those simple words. "I can't be with him like he is."

"Well, I, for one, respect the hell out of you." Coral nodded. "It shows how strong you are not to succumb to your destiny."

"He regrets the way he acted, though." Amethyst leaned forward like she was telling me a secret. "So things are already set in motion."

She was like a fortune cookie. "How the hell do you know all this?"

"Amethyst here is an empath." Coral laid her head against the headrest. "She could feel the emotions between the two of you."

"Yeah, just like he doesn't hate us." Amethyst tapped her fingers on her legs. "He's scared of you and of us."

"What do you mean?" Why would he be scared? That made no sense.

"I can only tell you how he feels." She pursed her lips. "Not why."

The sound of a truck pulling into the driveway filled my ears. "They're here. Please don't say anything."

"No worries." Coral winked.

I turned, opened the front door, and went out to help them. I felt so damn bad that Jacob had gotten hurt. He'd been distracted because of me.

The truck door opened, and Jacob stood. "Hey." His brown eyes warmed when they met mine.

"Are you okay to walk?" He'd been so dizzy earlier. I didn't want him to fall and get hurt again.

"Yeah, I'm okay." He took my hand.

I wanted to pull away, but I couldn't. Not right now.

"Go on in." Samuel waved me off. "I'll grab his stuff."

Jacob and I walked hand in hand into the living room. I tugged him toward one of the love seats and sat down.

"You already look a lot better." Amethyst sounded optimistic. "I'm glad."

"Me too." Jacob wrapped an arm around my shoulders. "I was nervous they were going to try to take me to the hospital."

"Yeah, you got lucky." Beth sat across from us.

"Are you guys hungry?" Samuel asked as he and Finn breezed into the house. "We could order a pizza or something. Or is that not meaty enough for you?"

I wasn't sure if he was being a smart aleck or trying to be cute. "Actually, that sounds really good. We've only been eating on campus, so it would be a nice change."

Beth lifted her hand. "A supreme pizza for me."

"And we'll take two meats." Jacob reached for his wallet.

"This one is on us." Finn sat next to Beth. "Next time, you all can host us."

"As long as you're down for hanging out in a dorm room." Beth stuck out her tongue.

"I'll order it now." Amethyst walked off into the kitchen.

The evening was nice, and Jacob seemed more like himself. Still, we didn't want to take him back to the dorm and have the coach find out we hadn't kept an eye on him.

Amethyst came back downstairs with three pillows and blankets. "Sorry we don't have a spare room."

"Yeah, there's only two bedrooms upstairs, so we have a room for the guys and one for the girls." Coral grabbed a pillow and a set of sheets.

Jacob came out of the restroom and saw us getting the couches ready. I glanced at the clock and noticed it was close to midnight. It had been nice hanging out with them and watching television.

Within minutes, Beth claimed one love seat, and I claimed the other, leaving the bigger couch for Jacob.

We all got comfortable and turned the lights out after the witches had made it upstairs.

Beth's breathing soon steadied, and Jacob tiptoed over to me. "Hey, Emma."

I tried to pretend I was asleep, but he put his hand on my shoulder and shook me. "Emma?"

There was no way I was getting out of this conversation. I turned toward him. "Yeah?"

He rubbed the back of his neck. "Can we go outside and talk for a second?"

I had a feeling I knew what about. "Why don't we talk tomorrow? I'd hate to wake the others." I was being a coward, but I knew what I needed to do, and I'd been dreading it.

"Look, I need to talk to you tonight." He licked his bottom lip and huffed. "It's been driving me crazy."

Even though I dreaded it, it was a fair request. I had hoped to be a coward for a little longer. "Okay."

I got up and followed him through the kitchen to the back door. Their kitchen wasn't large and had outdated cabinets, but they'd painted them white and had flowers sitting on the rectangle table, giving it a homey feel.

The backyard had a small wooden fence that separated their property from their neighbor's. A small herb garden grew to the side of the yard with a wooden bench right next to it.

We were going to be out here for more than a few minutes, so I headed over and sat down. I tipped my face toward the sky. A faint breeze blew the smell of fall across the yard.

"You're so damn beautiful." Jacob sat next to me, his eyes glued to my face. "I'm so lucky to call you mine."

It was extremely possessive, and I didn't like it one bit. "I'm my own person."

"Oh, I know." He took my hand. "I just meant as my girl."

No, he hadn't. I was beginning to realize I was a piece of property he wanted to claim... a trophy.

An awkward silence descended between us.

After a moment, he blew out a breath. "Why was he there?"

I could have been difficult and asked who, but it wouldn't change where the conversation was heading. "I don't know."

"He always has his eyes on you," he growled. "Why won't he back off?"

There was nothing I wanted to say to that.

Jacob glanced at me again. "So you have no clue why he was there?"

"You just asked that question a second ago, Jacob." He was getting on my nerves. "My answer is the same. I don't know why."

"You've got to give me something." He ran a hand over his face. "Here I am, playing at the homecoming game ... You should be on the cheer team, Emma. Then tonight would've gone differently."

"I don't want to cheer." He wasn't listening. "How many times do I have to say it?" It was always about what he wanted, and when he didn't get his damn way, he'd call my parents.

"It's not like it's a huge deal." He dropped his hands into his lap. "We'd get to ride to all the games together and hang out a little on the sidelines."

"It's not happening." He was usually at least somewhat considerate, but it was like he couldn't see past his own desires in that moment. "And even if I wanted to, the cheer team is full."

"I could ask around and see if there's a way." His eyes brightened. "Or the dance team. I bet that one would be easy to get on to, and they travel with us as well."

"Jacob, I don't want to do either." This was further proof that I'd lost myself. My pack, friends, and boyfriend didn't see the real me. "I want to do dance for my own enjoyment and not for a football team or anyone else."

"No, I get it." He groaned. "But how the hell do I get him to leave you alone?"

That's what this was all about. His insecurities. I needed to stop being his rock and learn how to be one for myself. "Jacob, I can't do this anymore." He wanted me to be someone I wasn't. I'd been so wrapped up in losing Aidan that I didn't pay attention to what was going on around me.

His body stiffened, and he turned toward me. "What are you talking about?"

"You're pushing me to be someone I'm not." And at the end of the day, I wasn't being fair to him. I needed to figure out who the hell I was.

"Look, I'm sorry." He scooted closer. "I'm upset and acting out. Of course I want you to be yourself."

"I'm not even sure you see me." It was finally beginning to sink in. "You only see who you want me to be."

"God, no." He squeezed my hand. "All I've ever wanted is you."

"But I can't give you me when I haven't even figured out who I am." And whether I wanted to admit it or not, my heart belonged to someone else.

"Then, we'll figure it out together." He smiled, but his eyes seemed full of fear.

"No." I finally said the words I'd been too scared to say for the last two years. "We need a break."

"What? No." Jacob reached for my hand. "Look, I'm being stupid and jealous."

"You are, but that's not why." He deserved someone who was crazy about him. And no matter how I wished that person was me, it wasn't. "I just need some time to myself."

"Are you breaking up with me?" He sounded hurt.

"I don't know." I squeezed his hand.

"Then, don't answer that now." His shoulders sagged, and he stood from the bench. "Let's go get you some sleep. I should've waited to talk to you in the morning anyway."

"Okay." Sleep was good.

As we headed back into the house, I paused and looked upward at the moon. Realization was crashing down on me today. I wasn't sure if it was because of what had happened at the football game or if it was because my new friends were giving me a different perspective. But one thing was crystal clear.

I'd given my heart to Aidan four years ago, and now I had to figure out how to get part of it back.

CHAPTER TEN

I'd barely gotten any sleep last night. I'd tossed and turned on the loveseat the entire time, even after Jacob had dozed off. I had to make a change, but I wasn't sure how. There had to be a way for me to find happiness that wasn't reliant on anyone else. The last time I'd been truly happy was the night of Aidan's and my first kiss—well, until he'd run off and left me. That was flipping insane, and I wasn't sure what that said about me.

Maybe seeing Aidan again had given me a second chance. Maybe fate was wrong, and seeing him was meant to open my eyes again. Or maybe fate was just being cruel. Hell, who knew at this point?

Beth groaned and blinked a few times before looking at me. I wasn't sure what she saw on my face, but a sad smile filled hers.

If we'd been part of the same pack, we could have linked. It would've been amazing to have that capability right now, especially with Jacob less than five feet away.

Footsteps ambled down the stairs. It was obvious they were trying not to wake us.

Coral's red hair peeked out above the bottom step. She tiptoed across the floor, causing even louder creaks.

Jacob woke up, and soon, the three of us were staring at her.

"Damn wolves," she muttered. "I was trying not to wake you all." She wore a large, baggy shirt with skull tights underneath.

"Why are you damning us?" Beth sat up. "You're the one who can't be quiet."

"I was to quiet ..." She bobbed her head from side to side. "... ish."

"The only thing louder would've been you sliding down the stairs on your ass." Beth grinned, obviously enjoying giving her shit.

"You better be glad I liked you last night." Coral stood in front of the kitchen door, arms crossed. "That's the only reason I'm hesitating to kick your ass out." Her lips curved.

"Ladies, be nice." Amethyst's sweet voice filled the room as she glided down the stairs. "Maybe you two will play nice again once we've gotten some coffee in you." At the bottom of the stairs, the light hit her hair, making it glow. She was ethereal like an angel.

"Says the girl wearing unicorn pajamas." Coral stuck her tongue out.

I hadn't noticed it until she'd pointed it out. Amethyst had on a pink pajama shirt with a rainbow-haired unicorn and matching pants.

"I think they're cute." I was pretty sure Amethyst was the only one who could make them look cute.

"Thank you." With concern, she turned to Jacob. "Are you hurting this morning?"

"What? No." Jacob sat up and touched his head. "I actually feel normal now. Not dizzy or anything."

"Great." She sounded happy, but something had changed in her eyes.

"We probably need to get out of your hair." I hated that we'd put them out. "Don't you need to head to your coven this morning?"

"Yeah, we do, but we'll wind up having to wake the guys." Coral rolled her eyes. "They are a pain to get moving in the morning."

I grabbed my phone from the coffee table. It was nine in the morning. "Well, we'll get going." I stood and glanced down at my yoga pants and shirt.

"Let me grab the keys, and I'll take you." Amethyst walked into the kitchen, and the jangling of keys pierced the air.

Beth stood and stretched. "I'm not even gonna change. Hopefully, I can go back to sleep when we get there."

I folded up my blanket and laid it on the loveseat.

Jacob focused on me. "Maybe we could grab breakfast together?"

Of course, he'd ask in front of everyone. I didn't want to come off like an asshole, so I nodded. "Okay."

Amethyst entered the room again and headed to the front door. "All right, I'll go start the car."

The moment I turned to pick up my bag, Jacob took it.

"I've got it." He placed it on his shoulder.

It should have been endearing. He was trying to take care of me, but today, it rubbed me the wrong way. Without thanking him, I headed straight to the door. "Bye, Coral."

"See you soon, girl. And good luck," she replied.

"What's Emma's problem?" I heard Jacob whisper to Beth.

"You do realize she can still hear you, right?" Beth rolled her eyes as she followed me.

He sighed and stepped outside as I was climbing into the car. Beth got in the backseat with me, forcing Jacob to take the front.

Once the four of us had settled in the little car, Amethyst took off, catching me off guard. She zipped through the neighborhood, driving at least sixty.

That must have been what Coral had been referring to when she'd said *good luck*. I had thought she'd meant with Jacob.

Two minutes later, she slammed on the brakes, making them squeal, outside of Jacob's dorm.

"Uh ... thanks?" It sounded more like a question. "Once I check in with Prescott, I'll head your way."

I'd only met his roommate a couple of times, but he gave me a wide berth. There was no telling what Jacob had told him about me, but when a wolf claimed someone as a potential mate, single wolves backed off out of respect—well, unless they wanted to dispute the claim.

That right there proved he was a good, loyal friend to Jacob.

"Okay, see you then." Obviously, he either hadn't understood our conversation last night, or he wanted to push it further. Either possibility wasn't ideal, but he deserved the opportunity to talk more.

Amethyst popped the trunk, and Jacob moved around the car. He grabbed his bag and headed toward the dorm room.

"Be ready for an argument," Amethyst said and put the car in DRIVE.

"What do you mean?" It would help to get a little insight into how he was feeling.

"He's scared and desperate." She glanced in the rearview mirror. "That's a bad combination."

"Maybe I should join you for breakfast," Beth suggested. "I could be the buffer."

"There's no point." Even though taking the coward's way out sounded amazing, it probably wasn't the best strategy. "The conversation has to happen eventually."

"She's right." Amethyst nodded. "He won't let it go."

Great. "Any words of advice?" Maybe if she could impart some words of wisdom.

"Be strong." She took off toward the girls' dorm. "And stand your ground. He's hoping to talk you out of breaking up. And we both know this won't end well for him."

"Not for me either."

"Oh, please." Beth lightly slapped my shoulder. "We both know how this ends."

"Do we?" She seemed more confident than I did.

"Hell yeah, I do." She snorted, and there was a look of pride in her eye. "You're going to dominate both of them."

"I'm not into kink." I had to give her a hard time, but I couldn't believe her either. Aidan and Jacob were stronger than me.

"Maybe that's the problem, then." She grimaced and ground her teeth. "We both know I didn't mean it that way."

"There is strength inside you." Amethyst stopped the car and glanced over her shoulder. "You're meant to lead."

"A girl alpha?" That notion was absurd. I'd never met a strong alpha that was female.

"Oh, really?" Amethyst laughed. "Our priestess is always a woman, and then there's our legend of the star."

"The legend of the star?" I sounded like a parrot, but I'd never heard of it.

"It's likely an old wives' tale, but elderly members of our coven believe that one day, there will be an all-women council that destiny has chosen." She shrugged. "It sounds nice, but curses and prophecies always get things wrong. The one thing you can count on, though, is earth and the magic within."

"It does sound like an empowering story." Beth lifted her fist. "I mean, your race embraces the strength of a woman while shifters cast a blind eye."

"Eh, you can always dream," Amethyst said as I opened the door.

"Thanks for dropping us off." I needed time alone.

She popped the trunk as I approached it.

"No problem at all." She held her cell phone out the window. "What's your number? I can text you guys later. Maybe we can meet up for dinner or hang out this weekend?"

I rattled off my number and waved goodbye. "Drive safe and talk to you soon."

Beth and I were heading up the stairs when the eerie feeling settled over me again.

Aidan

IT WAS RIDICULOUS. I'd stayed out here all fucking night, waiting for her to come home. And of course, she'd show up with a witch, but at least, it wasn't him.

The longer she hung around the witches, the more fate would force our hand. The mark showed itself in her more with each encounter.

I stepped out from behind the building across the street from the girls' dorm, desperate to talk to her. I didn't know what I was going to say, but I had to hear her voice and be near her. I wanted to be the man she deserved so fucking much.

Emma

HE'D PULL this shit now. I turned around and found Aidan standing exactly where he had been last night.

Right when I began to turn back around, he called out, "Emma."

I paused but didn't reply.

"Please, I just need a minute." He almost sounded like the boy I remembered.

I had to remind myself he was manipulating me.

"Here, I'll take it inside." Beth grabbed my bag and pointed at Aidan. "One wrong move, and I'll be back down here to kick your ass."

He didn't say a word, instead keeping his focus on me.

Beth frowned and left me alone with him.

"What do you want?" I didn't want to shoot the shit with him. Being around him tugged at me in ways that made it difficult to clamp down.

"I'm sorry about last night." He sheepishly stared at the ground. "There's so much I want to say, but I can't."

"I've already told you that until you tell me why you disappeared on me, I'm not interested." I deserved to know.

"Look, I'd tell you if I could." He nibbled his bottom lip and blew out a breath. "You need to stay away from those witches."

"So that's why you're here." I should've known he didn't just want to see me. "Well, guess what, it's not happening."

"Witches can't be trusted." He stepped toward me and reached for my hand before stopping himself.

"Neither can you." I had trusted him at one point, and look where that had gotten me.

He winced, the words hitting him hard. "That's ... fair."

"All right, it was great talking to you." I'd turned to head back to the dorm when he grabbed my hand.

The buzzing sprang between us, and the connection began closing in.

No, I couldn't let the bond remove every sense of logic. I jerked my hand out of his grasp and frowned. "What, Aidan? What do you want to say? I won't stop being friends with them because you don't trust them. That's a bullshit reason, and you know it."

"There's more at stake than you realize." His golden eyes blazed.

"Then share." I lifted my arms. "I'm all ears."

"It's not that easy." His voice turned hard, and his hands clenched into fists. "I wish I could tell you everything. It's so damn hard."

"Nobody is stopping you." I pointed to the surrounding area. We were the only two out here.

"I'd betray my family." His body sagged, and he didn't seem so strong at that moment.

It pissed me off even more. He wanted me to feel sorry for him. He wanted to play the victim. "Then I'll save us both the heartache."

I spun around again, but he stepped in front of me, cutting off the way to the dorm. "Can't you just stay away from them for me?"

The wind picked up, and the scent of musk hit me hard. Jacob was here.

Aidan

THAT ASSHOLE WOULD SHOW up right when I'd been about to say "fuck it" and tell her everything. Maybe this was fate's way of telling me to keep my damn mouth shut. But if I did, her death could be imminent.

Emma

"GET THE HELL AWAY FROM HER," he said in a low growl and hurried over, stepping between me and Aidan.

"I'm here to talk to her." Aidan stood straight, emphasizing how much more muscular and taller he was than Jacob.

"She isn't interested." He sneered, and his brown eyes glowed slightly.

Great, they were here having a pissing match.

"How did you pick up on that?" Aidan chuckled. "You seem clueless with how uninterested she is in you."

"You're just jealous. We've been together for over two years." Jacob's jaw tensed. "Which is more than you can say."

"Guys, stop it." This was ridiculous, and their wolves were coming forward. If they weren't careful, they would shift right here. The last thing we needed was a human witnessing the whole thing go down.

"I'm not intimidated by that," Aidan said and shoved Jacob in the chest.

Jacob stumbled back a few steps and stopped. Then, he shoved Aidan back.

It was as if they hadn't heard me. "You two quit it."

They were so caught up with each other it was as if I didn't exist.

Jacob's nose flared. "You need to get a clue and leave my girl alone."

"She isn't yours," Aidan growled, and his eyes glowed like a flashlight.

"I don't belong to either of you," I said louder than I meant to.

They stopped and stepped away from each other.

"What the hell does that mean?" Jacob took a ragged breath. "I came to this school to be with you."

"And I didn't ask you to." In fact, I hadn't told him until the last minute where I was going.

"I stayed back at community college so we could be together your senior year." Jacob took a deep breath and pointed at Aidan. "He's causing this. Isn't he?"

"Didn't you hear me say she isn't yours?" Aidan smirked as if he had won the lottery or something.

"And I said I'm neither of yours." I couldn't get over how stupid they were acting.

"We didn't have a problem until he"—Jacob leered at Aidan—"showed up."

"Maybe that should tell you something. She was mine before she was yours." Aidan bared his teeth at him. "If my being around is causing her to look away from you, she wasn't yours, to begin with."

"Like hell, she wasn't, and don't even try lying. She was never yours." Jacob's breathing quickened, and he wrinkled his nose. "You've been stalking her. How sick is that?"

Then it sank in. They weren't paying attention to me. I spun on my heel and headed straight into the dorm. They could stay out there and fight each other. They didn't need me around. Neither one of them was my problem anymore.

CHAPTER ELEVEN

I woke up the next morning, tempted to not go to class. Aidan and Jacob had both been texting me nonstop yesterday. I'd never responded to either of them, so you'd think they'd get the point, but no. I'd shut down Jacob's and my mental link so he couldn't contact me that way. I checked my phone, only to find another twenty missed texts, mostly from Jacob, but Aidan had sent two.

Beth threw on her shirt and glanced at my phone. "Damn, I'm glad you put that on silent last night."

"Yeah, me too." I would've gotten no sleep otherwise. I centered myself and began putting concealer under my eyes. I had gotten some sleep last night, which was better than the night before.

"We need super-sized coffees today." Beth put on her black shirt over her black skirt.

"No kidding." I wanted to be a coward today and hide in my dorm. "It wouldn't be a big deal to skip class, would it?"

"Yes." She sat on her bed and put on her black commandos. "It would be a huge deal. You can't let those two idiots derail you."

"I mean, I'm tired."

"Girl, no." She stood and grabbed my arm, turning me in her direction. "You're stronger than this. Don't take the easy way out. It's not like it'd make it better anyway. It's inevitable that you're going to see both of them, and the longer you drag it out, the worse it'll be."

"Why do you have to make sense?" I did appreciate her honesty, but damn, I'd been hoping she'd coddle me.

"Because that's what good friends are for." She took the concealer from my hands and started applying it for me. "Besides, I'll be there with you during first period."

"True. You can be the buffer between me and Aidan in at least one class." Granted, he wasn't the one who would be the worst. Jacob seemed the most desperate out of the two. "He's the one I worry the least about."

"Jacob is the alpha's son, right?" Beth finished with the concealer and picked up my brush and foundation.

"Yeah." I wasn't sure how that all played into this.

"So he's used to getting his way." She attacked my hair with the brush. "You're a challenge to him. You aren't falling all over him like the other girls do, and he has to work hard to stay by your side."

Things might have been different if I hadn't met Aidan. "Maybe."

"You do realize your wolf begins seeking its mate at around fourteen?" She arched an eyebrow.

"No, I didn't realize that." You'd think that would be important information to know.

"It's not common knowledge anymore since fated mates aren't a regular occurrence." She put down the brush and grabbed some eyeshadow. "So, most shifters don't seem to remember that fact anymore. The only reason I do is because that's when my parents found each other."

"That must be why you want to find your own fated mate so badly." Things were starting to come together.

"I've seen first-hand how different they are from other couples." She lifted the brush to my eyes. I closed them.

"Wait, is that why I can't get over Aidan?" Had fate screwed me over long before I realized it?

"You said you kissed the night before your birthday." Her breath fanned against my face. "It makes sense."

It hit me. "I was already fourteen when we kissed."

"How old was Aidan?" she asked as she finished with the eyeshadow.

I sucked in a breath. "Holy shit. He turned fourteen two months before me."

"The bond started that night." Beth ran her fingers through her hair. "Damn."

"Then, why did he stay away?" That was the question I always came back to. Why had he left me?

"No clue." She took the mascara and opened it. "But it had to be just as hard on him as it was on you, if not worse. He felt the mates' connection with you longer. He had to have left for a pretty damn good reason."

"Not one he's willing to share with me." That made it hurt even worse.

"Look, if you think about it, what he's doing is making it harder." She began applying the mascara to my eyelashes. "He left you and then had to see you with a new man."

"It's not like that." I'd never felt drawn to Jacob, not like I did with Aidan. Even though I fought it, Aidan was everything I wanted and needed.

"Doesn't matter." She dropped the mascara and

grabbed a lip stain. "Jacob was close enough to have the title of boyfriend even if it was more of an illusion."

"Whose side are you on?" I pouted.

She applied the dark pink color on my lips. "Yours. Even though Aidan may be your fate, he hasn't acted like a mate should. He hasn't learned whatever lesson fate needs him to. So you're going to hold out."

"Didn't plan on giving in." I glanced in the mirror and was once again surprised by how well she'd done my makeup. She had a gift. This time, I looked more natural, and the makeup hid my tiredness.

"Good." She placed the tube on the table. "Then, let's go get some coffee and get to class."

Yeah ... I wasn't nearly as excited as she was.

Aidan

I woke up this morning, resolved to do what was right. She might be my fated, but destiny was intervening. We weren't meant to be together. I had to protect her from my pack, but I still hadn't figured out who my father's ally was here. And I needed to protect her from him before I could go back home.

I embraced the anger and hurt. It was the only way I would survive what I had to do next. It had damned near killed me to walk away from her before, so there was no telling whether I would survive this time.

Emma

THANKFULLY, we were the first two in class as usual. We took our normal seats, and I wished there was a way I could block Aidan from sitting near us. If I did, he'd know how much he bothered me, which would only inflate his ego more, so I forced myself to take a deep breath and calm down.

"It'll be okay," Beth said as she patted my shoulder.

"I know." There were only two ways this would go down. Either he'd want to talk, or he'd ignore me. The problem was that I wasn't sure which one it would be. And even worse, I wasn't sure which one I actually wanted.

My skin began to buzz, alerting me to his presence. "Here we go."

"Is he ..." Beth cut off her question as Aidan strode into the room.

His eyes flicked to mine, and he took his normal seat. "No witches around?"

Of course he'd be a dick. I should've known he would be. "Not yet, but that can change at any second." I wouldn't let him get to me. He'd done it for way too long.

"Obviously, he's not a good judge of character." Beth leaned back in her seat and scowled at him. "So we should align ourselves with anyone he dislikes."

"She proves my point, and she's not even a witch. You're surrounding yourself with people who can't help you." He didn't even look in her direction. "You don't know what you're up against, Angel."

This was the third time he'd used my old pet name, and he was purposely being an ass. "You're damn right about that. Had I known, maybe what happened four years ago never would've happened."

"It would have been better for both of us if it hadn't." His eyes darkened as he looked forward.

He had no clue how true those words were.

As soon as Composition was over, I headed to the door with Beth walking behind me.

"Are you going to be okay?" she asked so quietly that not even Aidan would hear.

I nodded, not wanting to make it obvious what she'd asked. "Aidan probably won't talk to me anyway."

"We'll see." She raised the hand that gripped her phone. "Call me if you need me."

"Of course." She'd become my best friend quickly, and I only now realized it. She was in my court, and I'd told her secrets I'd never told anyone else. Well ... other than Aidan.

We walked down the stairs together, and then she headed out the door while I headed to Precalculus. Right when we split in the stairwell, a hard, warm hand that felt like electricity clutched mine.

Aidan

Watching her walk out of the room with Beth was way harder than it should've been. The longer I was around her, the worse I felt about treating her like shit. It didn't help that my skin was sizzling and my wolf was surging forward.

She was mine, so why was it all so damn difficult?

Emma

"We need to talk." His voice was low, and the sound stirred things deep inside. "Now that your little protector is gone."

I needed to remove my hand from his, but I couldn't make myself. I spun around and lifted my chin. I could at least act defiant. "What? I thought we'd said everything we needed to."

"Look, there's a lot going on that you don't understand." Aidan's voice cracked with emotion as his eyes dropped to my lips.

Our bond was charging us. We wanted to be closer to each other.

He gazed at my lips.

Okay ... I hadn't been expecting that, but I needed something from him before I could go back there with him. "You're sounding like a broken record." I needed to pull back, but I couldn't. His lips were only millimeters from mine.

"You don't understand. It's imperative to distance yourself from your new friends." His face softened. "I don't want anything bad to happen."

"They're nice." I got that his pack didn't get along with witches, but that didn't mean they were all bad. There were just as many bad wolf shifters as bad witches. The extremists on either side gave the races a bad name. "I can't judge them based on the decisions of their ancestors."

"It's not about them being nice." He nibbled on his bottom lip, and he threaded his fingers with mine. My chest brushed against his. "They aren't safe."

"How so?" He couldn't throw down unjustified accusations.

"I can't tell you." He stomped his foot and his words held conviction. "I don't want anything to happen to you."

I wanted to close the distance between us so damn much. "Aidan, I can't. Not until I know why you left me."

His tone took on an edge. "Emma, we've gone over this."

No. He was using our bond to his advantage to get what he wanted. "The only thing happening right now is you messing with my mind." I found the strength to jerk my hand from his grasp. "You can't just act nice to manipulate me into listening to you."

"That's what you think I'm doing?" His face sharpened. Any trace of warmth had vanished.

It hadn't taken him long to lose the concerned-mate act. I guessed that's what happened when you called him out on his shit. "Well, look how quickly your brooding and moody self fell back into place."

"Why do I even bother trying to help you? Obviously, it can't be because I care." He laughed humorlessly.

"You've been an asshole to me since we ran into each other." I was done being the pushover. The girl who did whatever because she was unhappy. "If you cared, our relationship wouldn't have turned into this."

"Don't act like you're innocent." His voice grew louder. "You're the one who had a boyfriend come to college with you. I mean, it put many things into perspective for me. Really."

"Says the guy who left me without saying goodbye." We were causing a scene, but I didn't give a shit. There was a group of girls huddled together, watching us, and a few students standing at the nearby doorway, pretending not to listen. They could think what they wanted. "Was I supposed to pine for you for more than four years?"

Aidan's jaw clenched and his nostrils flared. "It might've been nice to see you a little bothered by it still."

We were finally having it out. "Sorry I tried to move

forward. How the hell was I supposed to know you hadn't moved on yourself?" The energy flowing between us was building. I wasn't sure if it was hate, love, rage, or all three. But right now, I wanted to kiss him and punch him in the face. My wolf howled, wanting to get out to either kill him or claim him. Either option wasn't viable at the moment.

"Okay." Coral's voice rang in my ears as she and Amethyst appeared right in front of us. Coral grabbed my arm, pulling me away from Aidan. "You need to calm down."

"Don't touch her." Aidan's voice was dark and tense.

"You both need to calm down." Amethyst stood in front of Aidan, her back to me. "Things are getting out of hand."

"Out of hand?" I asked, trying to comprehend what she meant.

"Your ..." Coral glanced from side to side and lowered her voice. "... animal."

Holy shit. I hadn't realized how close my wolf was to the surface. I closed my eyes for a moment, hoping to hide the glow.

The people who'd stopped to watch moved on, realizing the show was over.

"Thank you," I said. It made no sense that he had a problem with the very people who had helped us.

"No problem," Coral said, glancing over her shoulder at Amethyst and Aidan. "I could see the sparks, and I'm no empath."

That was just lovely.

"I've got to get to class." At least, we weren't right in front of the classroom. It was five feet away, but even if I'd wanted to pretend that no one in there had seen, I couldn't. "I'll see you after?"

"Yup, we'll be here." Coral nodded and patted Amethyst on her shoulder. "Let's get going."

Amethyst turned to check on me. "Okay, I think they'll be fine on their own, for now." She pulled me into a huge hug. "You're both hurting. He cares more than he lets on."

As the two of them walked down the hallway, I avoided Aidan's eyes and went straight to our class. A few moments later, he followed behind me and took his usual seat next to me.

"I'm sorry," he said so quietly I thought I'd imagined it.

I RUSHED out of Precalculus for two reasons. First, I didn't want Aidan to catch up to me, and second, I didn't want to run into Jacob like I normally did when he was heading to Composition II. Just as I was turning toward my dorm, thinking I was free and clear, Jacob stepped into my path several feet ahead of me.

"Emma!" Jacob hurried up to me. "I've been trying to call you and ..." He stopped and pointed to his head.

Discretion was not one of his strong suits. He was pointing out the mental block I'd put between us. Without responding, I tried to walk past him.

"Please." He took hold of my arm and tugged me toward him.

What was up with the two of them thinking it was okay to grab me? "I'm not interested in talking."

"I'm sorry about yesterday. Things got out of hand." Hurt filled his eyes. "I was being a dumbass."

"No argument here." I yanked my arm away and growled, "There's nothing to talk about. I told you I need a break."

His forehead lined with worry. "But we're still together, right?"

"Jacob, I'm not right for you." Didn't he see that I didn't care for him the way I should?

"Yes, you are." He placed his hands on my shoulders. "I've known it since your fourteenth birthday party."

Of course, the night I'd gotten my heart broken was when he'd felt it. "Then you're not right for me."

He jerked back. "What do you mean?"

"I mean you aren't my fated." I didn't want to hurt him, but he was forcing my hand here.

"Well, that's not likely to happen." He smiled like he thought I was being adorable. "But I can change. You only need to tell me how. Hell, even your parents want us together."

"That's the thing. I don't want to be with you." I would have to be cruel to end this.

"What?" His brows furrowed, and he sucked in a breath. "You don't want to be with me?"

"No, I don't." I couldn't show any vulnerability, or he'd try to push harder. "I haven't been happy for a while."

"But I thought..." He blinked several times.

"You're a great guy." That was the truth. "And you'll make someone very happy someday. But that person is not me."

"Emma, what the hell?" Coral hurried over and waved her finger from side to side. "I told you we'd meet you outside the classroom."

"Crap, I forgot all about that." I'd just wanted to get away from Aidan. Just thinking of him made a chill run down my spine.

I glanced and found him twenty-five feet away, leaning

against a tree as he watched my exchange with Jacob. He was wearing a smug grin on his face.

Great. He had to think I was breaking up with Jacob because of him.

I stomped over to him and pushed my finger into his chest. "Don't be so smug, asshole." I came so damn close to growling at Aidan. "I don't want you either." Electricity coursed through us, but I ignored it.

The smile fell from his face, and fear flickered in his eyes. "Emma." His voice was low and held promise.

"Now, let's go grab lunch." Coral looped her arm in mine, pulling me away from Aidan. "Food might do us all some good."

We headed toward Jacob, who looked broken. His eyes were glassy as if he might cry, and he watched as we walked by.

"Emma," Aidan called behind me, but I didn't give a damn.

We reached Amethyst, who placed her hand on my arm, dragging me toward the Student Center. She called over her shoulder, "Glad you're feeling better, Jacob. We'll see you around."

These two girls had saved me twice within an hour. I at least owed them a cup of coffee. I glanced back to find Aidan still watching me. He looked broken, too.

Aidan

FEAR CIRCULATED THROUGHOUT MY BODY. I'd never felt petrified before, but I did now. I'd fucked up and so badly.

She wouldn't stop hanging around the witches, and I

didn't have the strength to walk away from her again. I'd been stupid to think I could.

Why had it taken until now for me to realize I couldn't lose her? Had I lost her already? She didn't need me anymore. She'd finally realized she was strong enough to make it on her own, but dammit, I couldn't live without her.

I had to try one last thing and pray to the gods I wasn't too late.

CHAPTER TWELVE

Emma

The three of us headed into the Student Center to grab lunch. My phone buzzed, and I considered not even checking it, figuring it would be Jacob. However, Beth's name popped up on the screen.

I just passed Jacob. Where the hell are you?

Great. I typed out my response: **In the Student Center with Coral and Amethyst.**

Her response was immediate. **On my way.**

"Now, what do you want to eat?" Amethyst smiled as her eyes sparkled.

"I still don't see how you're so skinny." Coral adjusted the bag on her shoulder.

"Oh, be nice." Amethyst waved her off. "I'll go get us each a latte and some cookies. I'll be right back." She danced off toward the cafe.

"How is she always so happy?" Granted, I'd only been

around her a handful of times, but there was this sweet, happy soul inside her.

"That's just her." Coral waved me over to a corner table. "Enough about her. Let's talk about what went down out there."

I laughed. That probably wasn't a normal reaction toward someone who'd just broken up with her boyfriend of two years. "Let's wait. I'd rather tell the story once. Beth is on her way, and I'm sure Amethyst will want to hear it as well."

"Well, fine." She crossed her legs and lifted her pointer finger. "But, I'll have you know patience is not my virtue."

"I guess I'll help you out with that flaw, then." Hanging out with them felt so natural. Even though Aidan thought I was making a huge mistake, I wasn't.

"Oh, look at you." Coral laughed as she sat at the round table and pulled out the chair beside her for me.

As I sat, Beth came rushing up. Her eyes widened, and she pointed right at me. "What is going on?"

"Here we go." Amethyst carried a drink carrier with four lattes and a bag of cookies. "Now, we're ready to hear it."

"You caught over half of it." Those two had gotten me out of a potentially awkward situation with Jacob.

"Well, I caught none ... other than Jacob rambling that he had to get home." Beth threw her bag on the ground and sat next to me.

"Thank you," I said, taking my latte, and glanced at the three girls staring at me, ready for me to begin. "I mean, I broke up with him." There really wasn't more to the story than that.

Coral ran her finger across the table. "Well, that's obvious, but why?"

"We all know she isn't into him." Amethyst took a large sip of her drink and put it down. "Otherwise, she'd be freaking out right now."

Coral grabbed her drink too. "So, why does he want to go home?"

The reason was crystal clear to me. "He wants to tell his dad and my parents."

Beth rubbed her temples. "Why?"

"Because his dad is the alpha." I hoped I was wrong. Jacob surely wouldn't be going home to get my parents and his dad to try to force us back together. That would be messed up.

"He's acting like a child." Coral picked at her cup. "Will your parents get involved?"

"Maybe, but they'll support whatever decision I make." Mom had pulled me aside before we'd come here. She'd noticed I wasn't happy, and she'd apologized for any part she'd had in it. She'd said that no matter what, she was on my side. She must have realized how I felt about Jacob.

"There is that." Amethyst gave me a sad smile. "I do hate it. He is hurting really bad."

"Hell, I picked up on it the night of the game. I could see you weren't nearly as into him as he was into you." Coral flipped her hair over her shoulder. "He didn't care as long as you stayed with him."

"He brought up that I'm the only reason he decided to come here." I couldn't feel bad about that. I'd never asked him to do that. In fact, I'd told him not to come to Crawford if he was only coming because of me. "You know what? It doesn't matter now. I want to move on." My skin buzzed, but I ignored it.

"Well, you might have a very hard time doing that." Beth snickered and took a sip of her coffee.

"What? Why?" I hadn't expected that from her.

"Because Aidan is over there, staring right at you." She pointed in his direction.

Of course he was. I shouldn't have ignored the buzzing that coursed across my skin. I turned, and our eyes locked. Standing at the door, he motioned for me to come to him. He mouthed the word "please."

Coral wrinkled her nose in disgust. "You don't have to go if you don't want to."

"He's her mate." Amethyst patted my arm. "You need to talk to him. He's heartbroken right now."

Beth glanced at Aidan and back to Amethyst. "You can feel that from across the room?"

"Well, yes ... faintly, but it was mainly when she told him she didn't want him either." Amethyst shrugged. "He was hurt and scared. I'd go talk to him."

I both wanted and didn't want to talk to him, but I'd regret it if I didn't try one last time.

"Let me know if you need me." Beth lifted her drink like a weapon. "Man or not, I'll make him hurt."

"And I love you for it." I picked my drink up from the table and headed over to him.

When I was a few feet from him, a group of people walked between us, keeping us separated for a little longer. Once they'd finally passed, he stepped toward me.

"Can we take a walk together?" Anxiety laced his voice.

He thought I might say no. He knew I wouldn't fall all over him like I used to. "You've got five minutes."

"Better than nothing." He opened the door and held it for me.

Nope, he wasn't going to get to be a gentleman all of a sudden. I moved to the door on the other side, opened it for myself, and headed out.

"Okay, then," he mumbled, following me outside.

I moved to the side of the doorway and stood on the stone pathway, under a tree. "What's up?"

"What's up?" He motioned between him and me. "That's what it has come to between us?"

"Oh, I'm sorry." I was already annoyed, and we were only a couple of sentences in. "Am I supposed to stroke your ego or tell you how desperate I am to have you by my side?"

"It wouldn't be a bad start." He winced and forced a grin.

"Yeah, goodbye." I'd turned toward the Student Center when he reached out and took my hand.

"I was kidding." His hand was gentle on my skin. He was allowing me to walk away if I wanted to.

For some stupid reason, it made me want to stay. "Then get to it." The buzzing between us hurt, but in such a damn good way.

"I miss you," he said low and full of meaning.

I glanced over my shoulder, expecting a cruel comment to come next, but what I found made the walls around my heart tremble.

No, I couldn't let one moment of kindness crumble everything I'd built up. I couldn't let him have that power over me. He had to earn it. "And you just realized that now?"

"Not exactly." He took in a deep breath and stared at the ground.

We were the only two out here now since everyone was either in class or inside the Student Center.

"You've been an asshole." If he thought I wouldn't call him out on his shit, he would learn otherwise and fast.

"I have." He rubbed his free hand down his face. "You're right, but there is a reason for it."

"I'm listening." I turned around and leaned against the tree trunk.

"It's for the same reason I left that night." He nibbled on his lip.

It bothered me that I still didn't know why he'd left after all that time. He wanted to tell me something but wasn't sure if he should or how.

"Which is...?" I wasn't getting my hopes up. He always shut me down when we got to this point in the conversation.

"There's something at play here." He dropped my hand and ran both hands through his hair. "Something bigger than you and me."

"And ..." Did he think I would be okay with that?

"I left that night to protect you." His golden eyes glowed ever so slightly as his wolf surged forward.

"From what?"

"Look, our being together will force my hand at something." His shoulders sagged, and he lifted a hand in front of him.

"I would never force you into something." That didn't make any sense. "Have I ever made you think that before?"

"It's not you who's doing it." He groaned and glanced around again like he was expecting someone to appear. He took my hand and tugged me to a bench on the other side of the tree. He sat down and nudged me to sit down too. "Today, you scared me."

I hadn't expected him to admit something like that so easily. "What do you mean?"

"When you told me you didn't want me either, I realized you meant it." He blew out a breath and looked deep into my eyes. "And I'm hoping I'm not too late."

"Just tell me what the hell is going on." I was so tired of

him keeping me in the dark. "How does our being together result in you having to make some sort of choice?"

He leaned closer to me. "I can't tell you that right now, but I've been protecting you."

"From what?" The only person I needed protection from was him. "All you've done is hurt me. Do you know what it was like the night of my birthday? I ran to the border, ready to see you. I kept reliving that kiss over and over in my mind, and you never showed. You didn't even say goodbye."

"My family will reject me, Emma." His hands fisted at his side. "That night, I realized what they would do if they found out about you. I couldn't allow it to happen."

"Because I'm from the enemy pack?" Could it be that simple? He was torn between me and his family?

"In a way, yes." He reached up and touched my cheek. My eyes closed of their own accord. His fingertips zapped my skin, and my breathing became ragged. "I can't tell you everything yet. I need time, but what I do know is that I never want to lose you. It took until today for me to see how close I came to actually doing that."

"I can't do this. If there's a chance that you'll walk away again, I need you to do it now."

"There isn't." His minty breath filled my senses. "But I need your patience as I figure out what to do. Now that I'm away from them, we can be together without causing problems. But I still have to handle this very delicately before I can tell you everything. Can you be patient for a little while longer?"

"I don't know ..." I wanted to be with him more than anything, but I didn't want to set myself up for more heartache.

"I promise you are it for me. Even if it means walking away from my family." He wrapped his other hand around the back of my neck. "But I need to get certain things in place first."

He was telling the truth. The signature stench of a lie was missing. The air was clear, and no trace of rotten eggs filled my nose. But maybe this was all a little too late. "I don't know..." If he hurt me a second time, I wouldn't survive it.

"I deserve that." He blew out a breath and moved, removing his wallet from his back pocket. "This probably doesn't change anything, but I need you to know that I never stopped thinking about you... loving you even when I came off like a douche." He pulled out some pictures.

"What?" I blinked a few times not believing what I saw. They were of me. One was at a football game cheering--I was on top of the pyramid. Another one was of me right outside my school in my prom dress. Jacob had his arm around me. "Where did you get these?"

"I took them." He closed his eyes and his cheeks turned a slight pink. "I always watched when I could to make sure you were safe. Do you remember that night of prom when you left and there were lilies on your car?"

"Yeah." Jacob had said he'd put them there. I'd be so surprised that he remembered my favorite flowers.

"They were from me." He barked out a humorless laugh. "But that prick took credit, and you believed him."

"I thought I smelled your scent but that I was going crazy." When Jacob said it had been from him, I was afraid not to believe him. Maybe he had done everything, thinking he was protecting me. "I'm willing to try again as long as you promise to tell me everything soon."

"Promise." He focused on my lips, and he scooted even closer to me.

My heart began to race. There was no hiding it, and when he lowered his head, my brain became foggy.

His lips touched mine, and an electric jolt shot through me. Until this very moment, I'd never understood what people meant when they'd said it hurt so good. I licked his lips, needing to taste him.

A low growl emanated from his chest, and his mouth quickly opened to deepen our kiss. We both panted as we tried to get our fill of each other. It had been four very long years since anything had ever come close to this.

Just as I was about to lose all sense, I pulled back, creating a small space between us. "Someone could walk by."

"So what? You're mine now, and dammit, I've always been yours." He pulled me close so our lips touched once more.

A low moan escaped me as the musky scent of his arousal mixed with mine. My wolf took over, wanting me to climb him and claim him right here. It took every ounce of willpower I had to keep my human senses in control. We were in public after all; however, my wolf didn't give a damn.

My hands slid under his shirt, touching his rock-hard abs.

He pulled back and growled. "You're going to be the death of me."

"You're the one who didn't want to stop." I ran my finger along the waistband of his jeans as my lips touched his again.

A branch broke in the distance, and Aidan went still. He stiffened and scanned the area.

"What's wrong?" I spoke in a whisper so that only he could hear me.

"I've got to go check something." His jaw clenched. "Can I take you to dinner tonight?"

"Uh ... sure." My brain was trying to catch up to my hormones.

"Great." He squeezed my hand lovingly and stood. "I'll be by around six. Does that work?"

"Yeah." I hated that he hadn't told me what was wrong, but now wasn't the time to pressure him.

"Okay, I'll see you soon." He growled in obvious frustration as he pecked my lips once more. "Bye."

"Bye," I said faintly as I watched him hurry off in the direction of the sound.

"Wow, I'm going to say I wasn't expecting to get a show when we came out here to check on you." Laughter laced Beth's voice. "So ... I'm assuming that went well?"

I spun around to find them a few feet away from the main doors, staring straight at me. Oh my God. How had neither one of us noticed they were watching us? "It went ... okay."

Coral laughed. "If that's what okay looks like, I'm afraid of what *great* means."

"They are both happy." Amethyst smiled and waved them off. "Just ignore them."

I wanted to enjoy the moment, but something was bugging Aidan. I had a feeling it had to do with his family and whatever secret he was keeping. I'd be patient for now, but sooner or later, I was determined to find out the truth.

Aidan

SOMEONE near the tree line was watching Emma and me. This couldn't be a good sign. I tapped into my wolf and headed to where they were. They weren't even trying to run away.

I stepped into the woods right as a guy my age appeared from behind a tree. He wore a Crawford University shirt, and his soulless brown eyes found mine.

"Aren't you supposed to be investigating her, not making out with her?" The guy frowned as the breeze ruffled his brown hair.

"Ah... I take it you're the ally who's attending here?" I had no clue which pack he belonged to or who he was. He'd come here to check out the marked girl just like me, but he never reached out to me like expected. Dad figured that the ally decided not to come to the school after all since our pack was the stronger one. We were directly descended from the original Murphy alpha, and others didn't like being second place.

"Yeah, and thanks, by the way." He glowered. "Now I'll have to deal with a sobbing Rogers wolf crying over her dumping his ass."

That wasn't my problem. "Avoid him."

"I can't. He's my fucking roommate." He paced and grimaced. "Maybe I can actually get some information from him now since he won't be so shoved up her ass."

"What do you mean?" I wanted to say she didn't have a mark, but he'd know if I lied. "She's harmless. In fact, I was thinking about heading home." Those weren't lies.

"I think I saw something the other day." Hatred filled his eyes. "So you better check again. I'd hate for your feelings to cloud your judgment. I'd hate to have to call your father."

And the cards were out on the table. "No, I'm fine."

For the first time ever, my eyes were open. I just had to protect her.

CHAPTER THIRTEEN

Emma

My heart pounded as the clock ticked closer to six. I'd been ready for half an hour, and my hands were sweaty.

I'd gotten the call from my parents two hours ago. Jacob had informed them of our breakup. Like I'd expected, Mom wasn't surprised. They'd both told me that my happiness was the most important thing to them. It was good to know they were on my side.

"You need to calm down." Beth sat on her bed and glanced up from her phone. "You're going to ruin the hard work I put into your face."

"Hey." In her defense, she had spent thirty minutes making sure my face looked perfect. She'd done light smoky eyes that complemented natural pink lipstick. I'd tried doing it myself, but my hands had shaken with nerves. I felt like I was going on my first official date, and in a way, I kind of was ... if he showed. "That's harsh."

"Oh, stop." She rolled her eyes and scooched back on

the bed so her back was against the plain white wall. "You know you're gorgeous. I only meant your natural look will start melting if you don't take it down a notch."

"You're right." I was being ridiculous. My anxiety attack wouldn't force him to appear. I stood in front of the mirror and looked at my outfit. It was the thirtieth of September and still hot as fuck in the south. I had made it a point not to look dressed up. I wore jeans with a black shirt that was sheer from my breasts upward. I'd paired it with strappy black sandals.

I ran my hands through my straight blonde hair and glanced in the mirror. I was trying to retain a calm presence, or my heart would be racing before I walked out the door. "I'm just nervous. I mean ...what if he doesn't ..."

"Show?" She smiled. "Honestly, I get why you're worried, but I promise he will be here. Even when he was being an ass, he looked at you like you hung the moon."

"Were we looking at the same person? Because that's definitely not the vibe I got." His looks had been full of animosity.

"He only looked like that when you weren't paying attention." Beth placed her phone on the bed and gave me her full attention. "It was when he wasn't being guarded with you."

"Why do you think he's not being honest with me?" Was I making a mistake doing this? He'd meant it when he'd said he'd tell me what was going on when he could, but should I have held off on a date until then?

"Look, he's been an asshole." Beth lifted her hands to validate her points. "Honestly, I'm not a huge fan of his. But I'm softening to him. For him to look at you the way he does and act like an ass in the same breath means he's struggling with something. And for your sake, I think you need to give him one more chance. I'm afraid you'll regret it if you don't."

"But what if it shatters me?" I said softly, letting her in on my biggest fear. "It's like I'm jumping from one guy to the next."

"He won't, and we both know you aren't. You weren't romantically invested in Jacob. This isn't like you're suffering from a major heartbreak and jumping into a rebound relationship. Aidan is your fated mate. There's no getting around that, and let's be real... you both wasted so much damn time." Beth moved so she could reach me and gently touched my hand. "And besides, you're stronger than you give yourself credit for. Everyone sees it but you. Hell, you scared the shit out of Aidan because you were ready to walk away. If he lets you down, you'll pick the pieces back up, and hell hath no fury like a woman scorned."

"Really? You're going with the cheesy old saying?" I couldn't hold back the smile that was spreading across my face.

"Hey, I can't be held accountable for what comes out of my mouth." She pretended to scowl. "But seriously, no matter what happens, you'll be fine."

I wished I had the same confidence in myself as she did. "I hope you're right."

A knock at the door startled me. I'd been so anxious about him getting here that when he did, it scared the shit out of me. My emotions were a mess. I felt like a yo-yo.

Beth chuckled at me, wide-eyed and frozen in place. "Aren't you going to answer it?"

"Oh, yeah." I took me a few seconds before I could force my legs to move toward the door. Now that he was here, I was petrified.

As my hand touched the doorknob, my heart pounded

loudly in my ears. I could already smell his signature piney scent, and it made me dizzy. I forced a slow breath before opening the door.

It was a good thing I had, or drool would've been pooling at the corners of my mouth.

Aidan's dark, short hair was fixed into that messy, sexy-as-hell style, and he wore a brown polo shirt that molded to his muscles and somehow made his eyes seem more golden. He wore jeans similar to mine, the kind that fit instead of the baggy ones some guys preferred. His eyes went straight to my lips. "Hey."

I'd licked my bottom lip before I could catch myself. "Hi."

"Oh, dear God," Beth grumbled. "I can smell you guys from here, and that's saying something."

I should've been embarrassed, but I couldn't bring myself to care. I stepped into him as his arms circled my waist, causing my skin to buzz.

He lowered his head, placing his lips on mine and intensifying our bond even more. I licked his lips, which were now one of my all-time favorite things.

A moan escaped him as he opened his mouth, responding to each one of my strokes.

"Seriously? I might get pregnant just being near you two," Beth muttered as she sat back on the bed. "You do realize that not only am I getting to watch my second show of the day, but everyone in the hallway is getting one too."

That was equivalent to dumping cold water all over me. I pulled back slightly and smiled at him. "She's right."

"So what?" He grinned and winked at me. He released his hold on my waist but took my hand. His eyes scanned my body. "Are you ready to go?"

"Sure." I turned around to grab my purse and phone. "Are we going to the Student Center?"

"Nah, I figured we could eat off campus." He nibbled his bottom lip. "But if you don't want to ..."

"No, that sounds perfect." I'd only eaten off campus for the away games. Jacob always wanted to eat at the Student Center with the rest of the football players, so it would be nice to get out for a change.

"Great." He stepped into the room and nodded at Beth. "Hey, how are you?"

Beth's eyebrow arched higher than I'd ever seen it. She pursed her lips. "Good. I don't think you've ever truly spoken to me before."

"Yeah, I'm sorry. I've been an ass." He grimaced as if it had been hard for him to admit.

"Eh, no sweat." She waved him off. "You two go and have a good time, but just know ..." She narrowed her eyes at him. "If you hurt her, I'll kick your ass."

"Duly noted." He placed a hand over his heart. "I don't plan on messing up this time."

"Good." Beth pointed to the door. "Get out of here before you two start kissing in front of me again. There is only so much I can take. Our new friends are meeting me for dinner, so I better get going."

I'd felt bad leaving Beth to fend for herself, so it was nice to know that Coral and Amethyst had made plans with her. "Okay, I won't be out super late."

Beth chuckled. "I'm not your mother."

"Fine. See you." I walked out the door and into the hallway. "You ready?"

"Hell, yeah." He walked beside me as we made our way to the front door.

"Damn, Emma." Caroline was in the common area like

usual with her group of friends. "Did you and Jacob break up?"

Aidan's hand tightened on mine.

"Uh ... yeah." She always made me feel very uncomfortable. She was nice but in that superficial way.

She turned to Aidan. "So you're dating?"

"I'm her boyfriend." Aidan's voice was deep and clear.

The fact that he wanted to make sure everyone knew he was mine excited me way too much. Those were words I'd never thought I'd hear him speak.

"Well, I admit you traded up." She ran a finger along her bottom lip. "You wouldn't care if I tried talking to Jacob, would you?"

Maybe I'd misread her. She actually seemed sincere.

Aidan's breath caught as if he were afraid of my response.

"It's fine." It weirded me out, giving someone else permission to date the guy I'd spent the last two years with, but we didn't have the same instant connection as I had with Aidan. Granted, he couldn't bond with her since she was a human, but still. Even if he dated another wolf, it wouldn't bother me. "He's free to date whomever he chooses."

I tugged on Aidan's hand and headed for the door. I wanted time with him without anyone distracting us.

His body was still tense as he followed me, and as soon as we walked outside and the door shut behind us, he turned to me. "If she was a wolf, would it bother you?"

"Nope, not at all," I said.

I'd moved to head toward the parking lot when he tugged me back toward him. Aidan's eyes hinted of his wolf as a faint glow appeared. "Weren't you with him for two years?"

"I was going through the motions." It sounded really bad when I said it out loud.

"You went through the motions with him?" His eyes glowed brighter. "I'm going to kill him."

"What?" It took a second for what he'd said to click. "No. We didn't have sex."

His body relaxed. "Really?"

"You'd know if I was lying." But that brought up a good point. "Have you?" I had a feeling his answer would hurt. If we'd never met, it would've been one thing, but to hear he'd slept with someone after us bonding at fourteen would wreck my soul. "You know what? Forget I asked." I turned around to head to the parking lot again, needing some distance.

"Emma." He kept his hold on my hand and moved to keep up. "Wait."

"Look, I don't want to know the answer." I was acting like a crazy person. I'd asked and taken it back like I was a fucking middle schooler. "Let's just ..."

"No, I haven't had sex either." A grin tugged at the corners of his mouth. "So you can stop freaking out."

"Really?" Jacob had always complained about a man having needs. He'd never pushed me to have sex, but he'd wanted other things.

"No one could hold a candle to you." He stepped into my space and cupped my cheek.

Now I understood how he'd felt when he'd learned I was still a virgin. "Thank God."

He leaned his forehead against mine. "We've been a mess."

"Yeah, we have been." Everything about this moment felt right. We were off at college and finally together.

This time, I initiated a kiss. I raised my head, connecting my lips to his.

His response surprised me. Instead of taking it slow and gentle like the other times, his lips brushed against mine, his tongue begging for entrance. I opened my mouth gladly, wound my arms around his neck, and plunged my hands into his hair.

The buzzing of my skin was on overdrive. Our chests touched, and his hands were tangled in my hair as well.

The door opened, and Beth's voice filled my ears. "Are you kidding me right now?"

A laugh bubbled out of me, and I pulled back from him.

"I thought you two were going out for dinner." Beth walked over and stopped. "Or is this what you consider dinner? I'm not sure you can live off each other's slobber."

"When you say it like that, it sounds really gross." My face hurt from smiling so much.

"No, it doesn't." He pulled me against him again. "Don't listen."

"Hey, you're still not on my good list." Beth wagged her finger at him. "So let's not push it."

"Do I have to be nice to her?" Aidan beamed as he waited for my response.

"Yes, you do." I smacked him on his arm. "That's my best friend."

Beth placed a hand on her waist and jutted her hip out.

"Fine," he growled.

"Let's go eat before we get in trouble." I intertwined our fingers and nodded at Beth. "See you in a couple of hours."

Aidan and I strolled toward the parking lot next to the girls' dorm. I was scanning the cars when I realized I had no clue what he drove.

"We're over here." He pointed to a new, black, Jeep Renegade. The car suited him perfectly.

It had a sunroof in the front and the back and black leather inside. He opened the passenger door, and I slid in. The car smelled new and like him.

He shut the door, hurried to the driver's side, and got in. He started the vehicle, and we were pulling out within seconds.

We sat in silence as he drove through the gate, and soon, he reached over the center console to take my hand.

It was strange. So much time had passed, but it was almost as if nothing had changed. When we were fourteen, we'd sit at the territory line in complete silence, enjoying each other's company. We were doing the same thing now.

We pulled into the parking lot of a small Mexican restaurant and parked near the front. The parking lot was full, and several college students were already here.

"It's a popular place, but they have the best fajitas around." He climbed out of the Jeep and hurried over to open my door.

When I stepped out, he pulled me into his chest and brushed his lips against mine. He whispered, "It's amazing and about damn time we got to be like this."

I nodded and kissed him one more time.

"Come on. I don't want people getting the wrong idea." He pulled away and smiled. "I want them to know I love all of you, inside and out."

The word *love* stopped me short, but I didn't want to say anything and ruin the moment by overanalyzing everything. We'd done that enough to last a lifetime.

We entered the restaurant, and the hostess smiled at us. "How many?" Her stand was against the wall, and a small hallway stretched left and right.

Aidan didn't take his eyes off me as he lifted two fingers in the air.

"Please follow me," she said and waved at us.

We turned down the right hallway and stepped into an open room with about six booths along the wall and ten tables. A large group occupied the corner that had several tables joined, but I didn't pay them any attention.

The hostess stopped at the fourth booth and laid two menus down. "Here you go." She turned and walked away.

I glanced at the designs on the booths. They were bright colors of red, blue, and green. Right as I was about to slide into one side of the booth, an all too familiar voice called out, "You've got to be fucking kidding me."

That's when I noticed Jacob with all his team members. Shit, he was supposed to be home. It figured our first date would end in catastrophe.

CHAPTER FOURTEEN

A idan took a protective step in front of me, which would only piss Jacob off more.

"I thought you'd gone home?" I cringed as soon as the words had left my mouth. That sounded like I was trying to sneak around, and Aidan must have thought the same thing because his shoulders stiffened.

"Oh, so you were hoping I wouldn't find out?" Jacob's normal warm brown eyes were black.

"No, that's not what I meant." Sometimes, I ran my mouth before thinking things through.

"Then what the fuck did you mean?" His words were cruel. He'd never talked to me like that before.

"You better watch how you speak to her," Aidan said with a trace of a growl.

"Don't tell me what to do," Jacob said and walked into Aidan's personal space.

Great, we were having another pissing contest. If I got peed on, I would never leave campus again.

"It's not cool how you're doing my man." Scott shook his

head in disappointment. "You kick him to the curb, and a few hours later, you're on a date?"

Of course, his buddies would gang up on me. Their camaraderie used to impress me, but not so much now. "He knew we were having problems. Don't paint him as the victim."

"We've always had our problems, but we've worked through them," Jacob begged. The hurt on his face was heartbreaking.

"It's been the same problem the entire time." How could we have worked through a problem if the problem never changed? "We were both ignoring the signs, but you're right. I should've been more honest."

A few of the other tables now stared at us.

I touched Aidan's arm. "Look, we're making a scene."

"Do not touch him in front of me," Jacob's deep and raspy voice sounded crazed, and his eyes glowed.

"She can do whatever she wants to me." Aidan straightened his shoulders, and the two idiots were almost chest to chest.

"Stop it." We had to take this outside before we got kicked out.

Jacob glared at me. "You don't get to tell me what to do anymore."

Hell, when had I ever told him what to do? I'd always tried to please him. Two waiters headed our way, and I could tell by their uncomfortable gait that they were coming to intervene.

They didn't have to. I'd take care of it myself.

I turned and headed straight to the front door.

"Emma, I'm not done talking to you," Jacob shouted. The tables that weren't close to us paused and turned in his direction.

It was hard to comprehend, but he really expected me to go back to him. He thought I was that trained. What was wrong with me? And it embarrassed me to realize how long it took to see how unhappy I'd been.

Their footsteps pounded behind me. I'd hoped that Jacob would stay put so Aidan and I could leave, but that wasn't happening.

I walked out the door and toward Aidan's car. I stopped and faced them. Aidan came over to stand next to me, and Jacob stood right in front of me.

Jacob's eyes were locked on mine. "Look, you're obviously going through something, and we can get through this. You don't need to get *him*," he said as he pointed at Aidan, "involved."

"She isn't yours." Aidan scowled at him. "She never was."

"Like hell she wasn't," Jacob snarled. "She was mine for over two years. Our bond is stronger than whatever demented thing you two have going on."

"I've already told you once; she was mine first." Aidan reached for my hand and paused as if he thought I might not accept it.

There was no way I could deny him. Maybe he'd had a harder time seeing Jacob and me together than I'd realized. I intertwined our fingers, and his hand squeezed mine lovingly.

"How could that even be possible?" Jacob focused on the way my hand was joined with Aidan's. "You bumped into each other once when you were young."

"That's not true." It was time I told him everything. He wouldn't give up otherwise.

Jacob paused and winced. "What do you mean?"

"Do you remember that night you found me on the border?" It was one of the most memorable nights of my life.

"The night of your fourteenth birthday party?" His brows furrowed, and he blinked a couple of times.

"Yeah, that's the night." I did hate hurting him, but there was no going back. The secret I shared with Aidan was coming out, at least on my side. "I'd been waiting for him." I glanced at Aidan.

"Wait ..." Jacob stared at the ground and tapped his foot. "You look just like the alpha of the Murphy pack. Are you his son?"

Aidan stiffened. "Yeah."

"So not only did he leave you alone on the border the night of your birthday, but he's the fucking son of the Murphy alpha." He lifted his hands toward me. "You can't be serious?"

That was news to me. Obviously, I knew which pack he was from, but I had no clue that he was their future leader. It finally explained why his parents would make him choose between his family and me. But right now, that didn't matter. Only two words could help Jacob come to some kind of understanding. "He's my fated mate."

If I'd thought he'd looked hurt before, I'd been wrong.

Jacob's body sagged. "How is that even possible?"

"We met each other when I was twelve." It was crazy to think how much time we'd wasted. "We've always felt a connection. It took him showing up here to make me understand why I've never gotten over him."

"So the whole time you were with me, you were pining for him." He slumped like the weight of the world crushed him. "We were good together."

"Because I went along with whatever you wanted." I

had to make him see it had never been a truly healthy relationship. "But I was never happy."

"I treated you well." He pointed at Aidan. "A hell of a lot better than he has."

"That's going to change." Aidan looked at me, a sad smile on his face. "I have many things to make up for, and I'll make up for them every damn day."

"You're both going to turn your backs on your packs?" Jacob lifted his chin. "Because they won't accept her, and I won't accept you."

"Are you being serious?" He was putting his foot down and acting like an alpha now? Of course, he would do it to hurt me.

"Yes, I am." His face hardened, and he glared at me. "If you stay with him, you won't be accepted by either pack."

"You're a fucking asshole." Aidan shook his head and clenched his fists. "You're trying to keep us apart."

"Call it what you want, but that's the final decision." Jacob shrugged, and a cruel smirk filled his face.

"Well, you're not the alpha yet." My wolf nudged forward. It'd been a while since I'd let her loose, and she wanted out real bad.

"Maybe not, but I'm stronger than you." Jacob's wolf surged, challenging me.

Scott stepped outside. "Dude, is everything all right out here?"

"Yeah, it's fine." Jacob's gaze stayed on me.

"I'll come out here with him," Prescott said and approached us. He wore a blue button-down shirt tucked into khaki pants. His light brown hair was short, and he arched an eyebrow, which brought out his light brown eyes. He stood next to Jacob, making it obvious they were the same height.

"Okay, we'll head back inside. Let us know if you need us." Scott hurried back inside, not understanding that his human instincts felt the animal in us.

"We were here first, Emma." Prescott stared me down. He didn't like me much, and the feeling was mutual.

He was the worst kind of douchebag. He came from money, and he was an alpha's son too. Even though he and Jacob were in competition, they were still a team and a quasi-pack, so he was willing to stand next to Jacob.

"That's fine. I've lost my appetite anyway." I turned to Aidan. "Let's go."

"Enjoy the little time you have." Jacob grinned at me and chuckled. "Fated or not, there's no way you two can be together."

"You listen here, asshole ..." Aidan started, but I held up a hand.

"I'll leave the pack if what you say is true." I was tired of him controlling and manipulating me.

"For what? Their pack?" Jacob crossed his arms and straightened his spine. "I already told you they won't accept you."

He'd gone from devastated to thinking he had the upper hand. Neither was a good look on the dickhead. "Then I'll figure out a third option."

"And leave your parents behind?"

"You can go to Hell." I let go of Aidan's hand and shoved my hands into his chest, making him fall back a step. "Unlike you, my parents love me unconditionally. All this time, I felt bad because I thought you were such a great guy. Thanks for making this so much easier." I spun on my heel and headed to the car.

Jacob's footsteps came charging. Then, I heard a dull impact and bone crunching.

I spun around and found Jacob on the ground, holding his nose as blood poured down his face.

Standing over him, Aidan snarled, "If you ever threaten her again, I won't be as nice."

"You better watch it, asshole," Prescott said as he got in Aidan's face. "I already warned you what would happen."

"Let's go." I hated that this had happened, but I was ready to go. "These dickheads aren't worth it."

Aidan was a couple of inches taller than Prescott and more muscular. Since Prescott wasn't technically being challenged, his wolf and pack stance wasn't being attacked. The only reason for him to be involved was to have his friend's back.

Even though I was talking to Aidan, he was still upset and didn't want to go. I walked over and took his hand again. "Let's go. Seriously."

"You're right." He blew out a breath and rolled his shoulders. "Let's go have a nice date."

I looked at Jacob and the blood coating his shirt. It served the asshole right. He groaned, playing up his injury.

If he thought I cared, he'd be surprised. I was done with him in every way, especially after tonight.

Aidan and I headed over to his Jeep, and once again, Aidan opened my door. I slid in, and within seconds, we were pulling out of the parking lot.

"I'm sorry about all that." I wasn't sure what else to say. Jacob had ruined our date.

"Hey, I'm not." Aidan took my hand. "I'm ecstatic that douche knows, but it pisses me off that he's trying to hold your family and pack against you."

"It's not a big deal, other than my parents." I shrugged. "I've never really felt like I belonged there."

"Now, that's something I'm familiar with." Aidan

frowned and gently squeezed my hand.

"Why didn't you tell me you were the alpha's son?" Now that we were away from the dickhead, hurt had settled in.

"I didn't want you to feel like we couldn't be together." He sighed and glanced at me. "But my older brother will take over the pack and not me. So it isn't a huge deal. Since I'm not expected to lead, it wasn't a super-important fact to share."

That made sense. That detail was irrelevant, other than his family being unwilling to compromise with our bond. "I understand, but it means we'll have to figure something out." I hated to think about it, but if his parents wouldn't accept me and my pack wouldn't accept him, our options were limited.

"We have time for that ..." He cringed. "At least a little bit. But don't worry. We'll figure it out together."

"I like the sound of that." And I really did.

"Well, is there somewhere else you want to eat?" His attention stayed fixed on the road as he drove.

"Let's go grab something at the Student Center." I didn't feel like being out now.

"Are you sure?" He gestured to the window. "We can go wherever you want."

"Maybe afterward, we can either go to your room or mine." I hadn't realized how sexually suggestive that sounded until the words had left my mouth. I should have been embarrassed, but damn, my wolf would be okay with him taking me in the backseat of his car in a parking lot.

He cleared his throat and took a deep breath. "As much as I want to take you up on that last part, we shouldn't put ourselves in that situation until I've figured a few things out. You deserve to know everything before you decide."

I wanted to argue with him and tell him it didn't matter, but I'd be lying. I needed to know why he'd stayed away from me for so long. Yes, I got that our packs were rivals, but my gut told me it was way more than that.

We spent the rest of the drive in silence.

"Are you sure you're okay with this?" he asked as we parked at the Student Center. "We can still go somewhere else."

"No, it's fine." The adventure of leaving campus had been a little too exciting. "Let's go grab a burger or something."

"Okay," he said and climbed out of the car.

I got out and met him at the back of the car.

"I was going to get the door for you." He took my hand, and we headed toward the large building.

"It's fine." I stepped into him so my arm brushed against his. "I promise."

Inside the Student Center, we found Beth, Finn, Samuel, Coral, and Amethyst sitting at a large table. They looked like they were only halfway into their meals.

When Beth saw us, her forehead creased with confusion.

Here was another test of our relationship tonight. "Hey, let's go talk to them for a second."

Aidan stiffened ever so slightly. "Okay, fine, but this proves I'm all-in."

I turned my body into his. "Promise to be nice."

He lowered his lips to mine and then pulled back. "Yes. Even though I don't like it, they seem awfully important to you."

"They're nice people."

We walked over, and Amethyst lifted a bite of her salad

to her lips. Once she noticed me, she dropped the fork on the plate. "Emma!"

Coral put down her sandwich and leaned back in her seat between Amethyst and Beth. She frowned at Aidan.

In her defense, he deserved it. He had been an ass to them.

"Are you here to insult us some more?" Coral angrily asked as Samuel and Finn turned in their seats to look at us.

"No, I'm not," Aidan said as he lifted our joined hands. "You're important to Emma, so that means something to me." He cleared his throat and ran his free hand down his neck. "I'm sorry for how I acted the last time we saw each other."

Samuel tilted his head and rubbed his hand along his face. "It's okay, man. It's how you were raised. Several wolf packs feel the same way you do. To be honest, I was shocked when Emma and Beth were nice to us. It's a breath of fresh air."

An adoring smile filled Aidan's face. "Yeah, Emma has a way of seeing the best in people."

"They may be willing to forgive you right away, but not me." Finn pointed his finger at Aidan. "Your kind holds grudges."

"He feels bad." Amethyst leaned across the table and touched Finn's arm. "He's being sincere."

"Until she's not around to hold him accountable." Finn removed her hand and stood.

"Hey, we're not sitting here." I hated to think he was leaving because of us. "We're going to grab something to eat and sit somewhere else."

"Fine." He sat back down, but his scowl remained firmly in place.

"Wait, I thought you were eating off campus." Beth

pursed her lips and picked up her burger.

"We ran into Jacob and the football team."

Her brows furrowed. "But he was going back home."

"Apparently, there was a change of plans." I stepped away from the tables and toward the food area. I didn't want Finn to try to leave again. "It didn't go well, so we came here."

"Well, I'll need the details later." Beth took a bite of her food.

"And us too." Coral snickered. "I have a feeling it'll be an entertaining story."

"I'm not sure that's the right word." I made my way to the food counter. "I'll see you all later."

"Bye," Aidan called out. After a few steps, he sighed. "I'm sorry about that."

"No, it's fine." I turned to him and rose onto my tiptoes so I could press my lips against his. "You thought you were protecting me, and now you're trying to make it right. He'll come around."

"I'll do whatever it takes as long as it makes you happy." He leaned down and kissed me again.

His words thrilled me. After tonight, I felt confident that we could make this work. Come hell or high water, we would be together.

I had two priorities, and both would be challenging. The first one was figuring out whatever was holding Aidan back. I wanted us to be honest with each other and choose our path together.

And the last one was understanding why Finn had reacted the way he had with Aidan. It was clear he carried some baggage. It would be nice for him and Aidan to get along since I felt like I'd already become friends with them. I was looking forward to finding out his story.

CHAPTER FIFTEEN

After Dance class, I walked out of the locker room and found Aidan leaning against the wall, looking downright delectable.

I couldn't blame all the girls for staring or glancing at him as they passed. He was, hands down, the most handsome guy I'd ever seen. Luckily, his golden eyes were locked on me.

He tilted his head, which emphasized his muscular shoulders. His casual black shirt fit him well in all the right places, and his jeans fit just right so the shirt outlined his abs perfectly.

"Hey, you." I probably still smelled sweaty, but the urge to kiss him was overwhelming. I pressed my lips to his.

As he responded to my kiss, he wrapped his arms around my waist and tugged me against his chest. He deepened our kiss and then pulled back. "If we don't stop, this could result in a very embarrassing situation for me."

"And you have a problem with that?" I'd never felt so free and flirty before. It was a nice feeling. Not only was I on a high from Dance class but from being with my fated mate as well.

"No, not really, but I don't want you to get a reputation." He brushed his fingertips against my cheek. "And that tank top and tight jeans are about to push me over the edge."

"Well then, my evil plan worked." That was totally a lie, but I'd take what I could get.

"You naughty girl," he growled, causing my body to warm and need to clench in my stomach.

Why did I like the way that sounded? I wasn't sure how much longer I could hold off from claiming him in all ways.

He'd leaned down to my lips once more when someone cleared her throat.

I pulled away to find my Dance professor crossing her arms and pursing her lips. She tsked. "I will admit he's a looker, but the school hallways aren't the place for foreplay."

Kill me now. I wanted to disappear, but that wasn't possible. "Noted."

Aidan's chest shook with laughter. "I apologize, ma'am. She makes me lose my head."

"We don't need any heads appearing, if you know what I mean." Her face was stern, and the message was clear.

I wished the Earth would split and swallow me whole. It took every ounce of willpower not to hide my face in his chest. "It won't happen again."

"Make sure it doesn't." She walked past us, her body stiff with anger.

"We better get to Chemistry before we're late." He chuckled as he took my hand and tugged me toward the door.

I was just glad he hadn't made a joke about starting Chemistry early or something like that. My face was on fire.

When we stepped outside, the slightly cool October air felt good against my body. I looped my arm with Aidan's, needing to get closer to him.

For the first time in my life, I felt completely happy. It was amazing how only a few days could change everything.

"Will I ever see you dance?" He grinned and stepped closer.

"Maybe ..." I ran a hand down his arm. "If you're lucky."

He grabbed my waist, tickling my sides.

"You better watch it." I slapped his hands away and pointed to the humans around us. "Can't you keep it together?"

"Not with you." His eyes glowed as his wolf snuck out.

The brick building came into sight, and I bumped my shoulder into his. "We're almost there, so you'd better get control."

"At least, I get to sit by you knowing you're mine today." He winked at me. "That makes the torture completely worth it."

"We'll see."

As we entered the building, my anxiety started to peak. I didn't know what would happen in the classroom. All I did know was that Jacob probably would be there and cause a scene. But I couldn't change that, and I couldn't rearrange my life to avoid him.

"Hey, it's going to be okay." Aidan squeezed my hand and directed us to the classroom. "You've got nothing to worry about."

"It's stupid, but his dad's my alpha." I needed to know

where I stood now that we'd broken up. I had to call my parents later and get a feel for what to expect.

"Doesn't matter." Aidan tucked a piece of my hair behind my ear. "We'll figure it out, and if it takes me punching that asshole's face again to drive the point home, it won't bother me any."

"I'm sure it won't." I laid my head on his shoulder. "I think you enjoyed it yesterday."

"Fuck yeah, I did." His minty breath hit my face. "That asshole thought he had rights to my girl."

As soon as we stepped into the room, I felt Jacob's eyes lock on us.

I turned my head in his direction and regretted it instantly. He was leaning against the table, his body turned toward the door, obviously waiting on us to come in. He tensed and pushed off the table, heading toward us.

Dark circles lined his eyes, and his brown hair was unkempt and, dare I say, greasy. His nose didn't have a huge bruise like it would have if he hadn't had shifter healing. However, his gray polo shirt was wrinkled, and his pants had some kind of stain on them.

"You couldn't find the class on your own?" Jacob slurred as if he were drunk. His breath reeked of wolfsbane.

"Have you lost your damn mind?" This wasn't going to go well. Wolves weren't supposed to get drunk near humans. It made them sloppy and could alert humans to the supernatural world.

"I'm mending a broken heart," he said as his voice increased in volume. "Not that you would understand since you moved on from me in a matter of hours."

"Dude, this isn't cool." Aidan let go of my hand and grabbed Jacob by the shoulder. "You're putting all of us at risk."

"Like you fucking care." He stumbled, forcing Aidan to steady him.

"We need to take him back to the dorm." I couldn't believe what I was seeing. I hated that I had hurt him, but he was being careless right now.

"Adam, tell them I'm fine," Jacob hollered at his teammate and almost tripped again.

"Dude, I think they might be right." He scratched the back of his neck and frowned at me. "You really aren't fit to be here."

"What the hell? We're teammates." Jacob pouted and turned his attention back to me. "See, you're ruining everything."

"Okay, it's time to go." I walked out the door, letting Aidan drag Jacob. I spun around to help, but it was already too late.

"Hey, I can walk on my own." Jacob jerked his arm from Aidan's grip and shoved Aidan.

Aidan didn't budge. That's how strong he was. It also helped that Jacob was hammered.

"Stop showing your ass." I still couldn't process that he'd come to class drunk. That was beyond reckless.

When we stepped outside, people stopped to watch Jacob stumble out the door.

As long as he wasn't fighting us, I was fine with it.

Aidan stayed beside him as I led us toward the dorm.

"How does it feel to break someone's heart?" Jacob's voice was barely louder than a whisper.

"Look, I'm sorry." I waited for him to catch up to me before continuing. "I never meant for it to happen."

He ran his hands through his hair and winced. "Did you ever care about me?"

"Of course I do." That wasn't a lie. I cared about him,

but I wasn't in love with him. Granted, his behavior wasn't helping his case. "You were one of the people I was closest to."

"You do?" Hope filled his eyes as Aidan growled behind us.

"Yes, but as a friend." That was the problem. I'd always cared for him as a friend. "I'm sorry, but there is someone out there who will feel that way about you. Honestly, you had no chance. I met my mate before you ever noticed me."

"Then, why did you date me for two fucking years?" Jacob sighed and rubbed his eyes.

"I didn't know Aidan was my mate, and you were always so considerate and sweet to me." He deserved answers. I could give him that. "I wanted to feel that way for you."

Aidan groaned and took a few steps away from me, making it clear he didn't like hearing it.

Well, it wasn't my fault, and he had to lie in the bed he'd made. I was having to face one of my biggest mistakes right now, and it was partly due to him.

Jacob reached out to take my hand. "So it wasn't all fake?"

"No, it wasn't." I dodged his hand, though. "But that doesn't change my decision. I'm sorry, but I'm not the one for you."

"What you really mean is I'm not the one for you." His laugh was humorless, and he scowled at Aidan. "He is."

"What do you want me to say?" We were getting closer to the dorms. I got that he needed this conversation, but it would have been better if he'd been sober.

"I just want to wake up from this nightmare." He frowned, and his shoulders slumped. "Not only do you not want me, but you want a fucking Murphy. They're assholes who want to take down anyone who doesn't agree with them."

That was true. Or at least that was what I'd heard.

"He's the alpha's son. Do you really think his father will let him walk away?" Jacob stumbled and reached for my hand again.

Aidan smacked his hand away and slipped between the two of us. "She's the most important person in the world to me. I will do right by her."

"Hey, I was talking to her, not you," Jacob moaned.

It sounded as if he was trying to growl. I wasn't quite sure.

"And I was giving you a moment to get closure even though I wanted to rip your head off." Aidan took my hand in his, making it evident that he planned to stay between me and Jacob. "But when you're trying to talk her out of being with me, that's when I cut in."

That was actually very fair. Even though he'd come off like an ass when we'd first run into each other again, I was realizing he was still the amazing boy I remembered, just a little older and maybe a little rougher around the edges, but that was fine with me.

Now the boys' dorm was only fifty feet away. "Are you good the rest of the way?"

Jacob paused before nodding. He started to say something but closed his mouth and headed toward the dorm.

"Oh, and Jacob." I'd make sure we were on the same page. "Another stunt like this, and I'll be calling your father."

He paused and then shook his head. "Fine." He continued on, and Aidan and I watched him until he went inside.

Aidan tapped his fingers along his thigh and shifted his

weight to one leg. "Do you know how hard that was to listen to?"

"I'm sorry, but I had to talk to him before he acted out more." I placed both my hands on his shoulders.

"That's the only reason I didn't put up a fight." He pulled me against his chest, and his eyes went to my lips. "Now I need to get the image of you and him out of my head."

If he thought I would protest, he was dead wrong. I didn't need any encouragement to help his cause. I grabbed his neck and slammed my lips on his.

He responded in earnest as his tongue met mine and the taste of him filled me. I could kiss him all damn day.

The tickling feeling against my spine broke through my haze. I pulled away, searching for the source.

"What's wrong?" Aidan's eyes followed mine.

"Something feels off." I'd thought it was Aidan, but if I was still having this feeling, he wasn't responsible for it.

"Really?" He took a few steps in front of me toward the trees. "I don't sense anything. Come on, let's go grab food at the Student Center since we're missing Chemistry."

"Yeah, okay." I hated ruining our moment, but the chill wasn't going away.

We headed back to the Student Center, and inside, I found Coral and Amethyst at the table closest to the door. I headed straight to them.

"Hey, you two are always together." It was worse than Beth and me.

"Yeah, we plan it that way. It's a little unsettling being around so many ..." Coral tapped her finger to her lips. "... normal people. We find it's comforting to have each other."

From what I'd heard about witches growing up, witches segregated themselves more from humans than shifters did.

Aidan nodded at them and pulled at his collar. "How are you two doing?'

He was so damn uncomfortable, but he was trying.

"Good, and you?" Amethyst took a sip of her coffee.

"Not bad at all." He turned his body toward them, making it clear they had his full attention, and took my hand.

"They're so cute." Amethyst clapped her hands twice. "I told you it would all work out."

"It's only, like, day two." Coral leaned back in her seat and crossed her arms. "Let's give it a week before you start saying you were right."

"Oh, it'll last. You know I can tell things." Amethyst stared right into my eyes. "He's in it for the long haul now." She pointed at Aidan as she looked at Coral. "And he wants to make things right with us."

Tensing, Aidan stepped back. "How the hell do you know that?"

"She's an empath." He hadn't been around when she'd informed Beth and me of that. "So..."

"That's damn unsettling." He ran a hand through his hair and pulled at his ear. "I mean ..."

"No, don't worry." Amethyst lifted a hand slowly and moved it side to side. "It's unsettling at first."

"At first?" Coral waved at her. "No, it's always unsettling. She knows how I feel before I do most of the time."

"I'm able to help you process it." Amethyst placed a hand on her chest. "It's sometimes a good thing." She pointed at Coral. "She has a temper."

Coral frowned. "As if they haven't figured that out."

The door opened, and the tingling feeling came over me again. I turned around and found someone who looked very similar to Aidan.

"So ...this is why my little brother hasn't finished his mission." The guy's voice was deep with disgust.

Aidan's jaw clenched. "Why don't we go outside to talk?"

"That suits me just fine." His brother's eyes were a dark gold, and a cruel smirk stretched across his face. "Why don't you bring her with us?"

"No." Aidan shook his head and touched my hand. "Stay here with them. I'll be right back." He stormed out the door, grabbing his brother's arm and dragging him outside.

Something wasn't right, and I had a feeling all of the secrets were about to be unburied.

Aidan

"What the hell are you doing here?" I wanted to mind speak with him, but humans were around, and we'd look weird.

"I got a call saying that my little brother might be thinking with something other than his head." Bradley glanced back into the Student Center where Emma was. "I'm inclined to agree."

"They're just trying to start shit." I had to find a way to make him go away, but I had no damn clue how.

CHAPTER SIXTEEN

Emma

I stayed back as requested, but something was wrong. I didn't have to be an empath to figure that one out. Did they somehow know who I was?

"This isn't good." Amethyst's words confirmed my fears. She took another sip of her coffee, and her hands shook.

"What do you mean?" Coral's forehead creased as she followed Amethyst's and my gaze. "It's two brothers talking."

"Fear is pouring off Aidan, and suspicion is pulsing off his brother." Amethyst rubbed her hands together. "I don't know what's going on, but it's not good."

"Should I go out there?" If Aidan was scared, I needed to stand beside him.

"I don't know." Amethyst's usual carefree demeanor wasn't present.

It freaked me out. That was one of the attributes I loved best about her. There weren't many people like her out there.

"Why don't you give them a few minutes, and if they still appear standoffish, maybe go then." Coral shrugged. "It probably didn't help that his brother caught him talking to us."

That was very true. If his brother took over the pack, that would include continuing the hatred of the witches and ... well, hell, me.

"Yeah, and Aidan was caught by surprise. That was what he was feeling before fear took over." Amethyst grabbed her coffee and took a larger sip.

"Then why would he show up here?" There had to be something we were missing.

"Girl, we know as much as you." Coral pointed in their direction. "But I'd be going out there if I were you."

I'd hate to make it worse, but knowing how he felt, I realized Coral was right. "I'll be back."

"Just holler if you need us," Coral called after me while she held up her hands and wiggled her fingers.

As I neared the doors, I could hear them clear as day due to my wolf senses.

"I come here and see you hanging out with a Rogers pack member and two witches." His brother's voice was rough and full of disbelief. "What universe did I walk in on?"

"Look, you asked me to come here and scope it out." Aidan lifted his hands in the air. "So I am. If I want real answers, I can't come in here all Hallowed Guild."

What in the hell was Hallowed Guild? I almost didn't want to go outside now.

"That doesn't mean you rub elbows with our sworn enemies, and you're obviously close to the girl. So what's the verdict?"

"Look, no one here is a risk," Aidan said slowly.

His brother took a step in his direction. "That's not what I asked."

Yeah, it was time for me to intervene. I opened the door as loudly as possible so no one could accuse me of trying to sneak out.

Aidan stared his brother down, and after a few seconds, his brother turned toward me.

His face was softer than Aidan's, and he even seemed less muscular. It surprised me since he was the alpha heir. Usually, they were bigger than anyone else in the pack. He must have been more cunning or ruthless.

"Hey, sorry to interrupt, but I wanted to ask what you wanted from the coffee shop." I smiled at Aidan and turned my attention to his brother. "Would you like something too?" I asked, hoping to play this right.

His brother took a step toward me and interlocked his fingers in front of his chest. "You do realize I'm a Murphy, right?"

"Sure do." I forced a bright smile. "But hey, we're away from the others, and it wouldn't hurt to be cordial."

"Our packs are natural enemies." His wolf emerged enough for his eyes to hint at a glow.

"Yet, we're here on neutral ground." I gestured to the buildings around us and shrugged. "If it's any consolation, I broke up with the Rogers alpha heir." Maybe that would count for something.

A small grin crossed his face, and he chuckled. "I can see why you're taken with her." He scanned me from head to toe, making me feel dirty.

"You better look away before I make you," Aidan growled.

"You're acting like she's your fated or something." His brother began to laugh, but when he took in Aidan's face, he stopped. "Holy shit. She is."

Aidan took my hand in his. "Yes, she is." He straightened his shoulders and nodded at me. "Emma, this is my older brother, Bradley. Bradley, this is Emma."

"I'd normally not be okay with this, but you have me intrigued." Bradley held his hand out to me. "It's nice to meet you."

Maybe we had a chance at being part of his family's pack. I couldn't prevent the hope from growing inside me. I shook his hand, making sure my grasp was strong. "Nice to meet you too. Do you want to join us for brunch?"

Bradley's eyes flicked toward the doors of the building. "No, but thanks. I have someone I need to meet up with while I'm in the area. Maybe we could have dinner?"

"No—" Aidan started, but I cut him off.

"Sure. Maybe I could bring my roommate." It'd be nice to have Beth there in case it got weird. I could always count on her.

"Is it another Rogers pack member?" Bradley's shoulders stiffened. "Because if so..."

"No, I'm not sure which pack she's from, but it's one in Alabama." I expected him to put up a fight.

"Then great." His brother smiled, but it didn't meet his eyes. "I'll be here around six to pick you three up."

"No, we'll meet you at the restaurant." Aidan's voice was cold, and he tugged me toward him. "Just text me closer to the time."

"Okay then." His brother walked around me, examining my face and neck.

It was weird and made me very uncomfortable. "See you soon."

"Let's go get that coffee." Aidan wrapped an arm around my waist, led me to the Student Center, and opened the door. As soon as we entered the building, he paused. "We need to talk. This isn't good."

"He seemed nice." Despite his strange perusal at the end.

"Do you really want a coffee?" he asked as Amethyst waved us over.

"It wouldn't hurt." I walked over to them, and Aidan followed behind me.

"Everything okay?" Coral grabbed a napkin and dabbed at her face.

"Yeah, I think so," I said as Aidan pulled me away.

"Can we catch up with you two later?" Aidan took a few more steps away from them. "I really need to talk to her."

"Oh, sure." Amethyst said as she gave Coral a look of warning. "Call us if you need anything."

"What's wrong?" Aidan's behavior gave me anxiety.

"You know when I said I needed time to figure out stuff before I could tell you all my secrets?" he asked as he headed to the coffee shop.

"Yeah." The truth was the one thing I'd been begging for.

"Well..." He started, but the cashier interrupted us.

"Hi, what can I get you today?"

"Uh... a grande vanilla latte for Emma," I said.

After he paid, he turned his focus back on me. "I've run out of time and need to tell you everything before we meet with my brother."

I'd been waiting on this information for the last four years of my life, but now that it was here, I had a feeling it would change everything. "Okay."

"Order for Emma," the barista called out.

I hurried over and grabbed my latte before turning back to him.

"Let's get out of here." Aidan took my hand and led me toward the woods at the back of the Student Center.

The area outside where we were headed was bare except for a handful of students hanging out around the benches in front of the building.

After we passed them, I didn't sense anyone else around between the building and the woods. Aidan scanned the area and led us about a hundred feet into the woods where the trees were thicker and animals ran around.

For him to take me this far out, it probably wasn't good news. "What's going on?"

"Look, this will sound crazy, but I need you to hear me out." Aidan turned toward me and took both my hands in his.

"Okay ..." I wasn't sure what he was about to tell me, but it couldn't be that crazy ... could it?

"The men of my pack and several other packs in the United States are part of a secret society."

"A secret society?" I'd heard there were several out there but never knew any involved shifters.

"Yes, only the men can be part of it," he said slowly as if this were a very important detail to understand.

"Why only men?" I was sure it was a very sexist reason. That's how all the men in packs thought.

"Because the women don't matter."

"Really?" This type of shit always pissed me off.

He lifted a hand. "Just please hear me out."

"Okay, so you're part of a secret society I can't belong to." It wasn't nearly as bad as he was making it out to be.

"That's not all." He nibbled his bottom lip and took a

steadying breath. "The society is searching for the cursed one. Our mission is to find her and destroy her."

"Her?" That was crazy. An all-male society was searching for a girl.

The sky darkened, making the woods feel like night time. The creatures quieted as if they were listening to his story.

"A long time ago ..." Aidan paused and ran a hand down his face. "... our alpha had a fling with a witch. The Rogers pack protected the witch in return for her healing powers. At that time, your pack and mine got along. The alpha was infatuated with her but knew such an abomination couldn't become his mate. When she became pregnant, he left her."

"She was good enough to sleep with but not commit to?" What the hell was wrong with people?

"I'm not saying what he did was right." He sucked in a breath. "The Rogers pack alpha came to our alpha one night and informed him that the witch was in labor. Our original alpha knew he had to do something, so he followed the Rogers alpha back to their territory and entered the witch's home."

"I have a feeling this doesn't have a happy ending."

"No, it doesn't." Aidan closed his eyes for a second before continuing. "Long story short, the witch couldn't survive birthing a shifter. It's not natural and can't happen except in rare occurrences. Even though she was the first, her connection with the earth informed her of her fate. When she realized the man she loved would kill her child, she did the only thing she could do to hurt him. She cursed him."

"Wait ... he killed his child?" What kind of asshole could kill their own child?

"Yes, but that's not what's important in this story." He

winced. "I didn't mean it like that. But you've got to understand that this secret society believes the original alpha did the right thing."

"Do you?" I hoped with everything inside me that he said what I wanted to hear. I wouldn't know what to do otherwise.

"I used to, but that changed when I kissed a girl at the border."

"But why did you leave me, then?" It always came back to that night between us.

"For you to understand my reason, I need to tell you the curse." He took my other hand again and stared deep into my eyes. "Every fifty to a hundred years, fate draws a male shifter to a female witch. When this happens, a girl is born from the union. She is part wolf and part witch. Her magic is hidden at first, but when her power releases, the curse is then set into motion. She is destined to lead the wolf packs. She is meant to be our leader."

"So, because he was an alpha asshole who thought of women as disposable, this was her way of getting even." It was cruelly just.

"Yes. Four different girls have been born of that curse. Each one was killed at eighteen before their powers set in." He stopped, and fear shone clear in his eyes.

"What does this have to do with us?" My mind was screaming at me, but I didn't want to listen.

"There are certain signs when one is born." He stepped toward me. "A dormant volcano becomes active, volcanic lightning streaks the skies, and a meteorite hits Earth. All those signs happened eighteen years ago."

Those were all things that had happened right before I was born. We'd learned about them in history class. I wanted to ask questions, but my mouth wasn't working.

"So when we saw the signs, we began our search for the one with a birthmark right behind her ear. History states that it looks like an incomplete star. With each woman who comes, the tattoo grows more complete. The one born eighteen years ago should have a full star since she's the fifth born of this curse. All five points would be connected."

My birthmark. I dropped his hand, and my fingers reached for the birthmark he spoke of. "No ..." It couldn't be. "That doesn't make any sense. A dead wolf lay beside me on the border."

"A male, right?" His eyes bored into mine. "So, where was the female?"

"This has to be some kind of joke." But his story resonated with me as though my soul had connected with it.

"It's not. That's why I left you that night." He ran his free hand through his hair, grabbing at his scalp. "When I put that necklace on you, I saw the mark."

"Then, why didn't you alert your family?" Obviously, he hadn't wanted to be with me, so why not finish the job?

"I told you why earlier. It's because I couldn't, and I needed to protect you. The more time I spent around you, the more my family would have taken notice." He stepped into me and cupped my cheek. "I walked away to save you."

"But you came here ..." It didn't make sense.

"First off, we can't kill the girl until she's eighteen. We refuse to attack children. And second, I thought by leaving you, you wouldn't be found. I had no clue who my target was when I came here. That is until I saw you."

"If you didn't tell them, how did they find out about me?" None of this made sense. "And why did the alpha kill the child if you aren't allowed to kill children? How is eighteen okay, and how many girls have you killed? And how did you know who to watch if you didn't know it was me?"

All my questions spilled out since my mouth had started working again.

"Those are fair questions." He rubbed his hands together. "As I said, once the signs are there, we begin looking for the mark on female shifters. Someone came to a high school football game when you were a cheerleader, and your hair was pulled into a ponytail. They caught a glimpse of something that could have been a birthmark. I was told it was the Rogers alpha's son's girl. I hadn't realized that the guy you were dating was the alpha heir until I saw you here with him."

Wow. Now that he'd said that, I remembered the particular tingling feeling at the homecoming game. I'd brushed it off, but now I knew it had meant something.

"As far as the alpha killing his child, his beast had begun controlling him more and more. When you let out your wolf to commit such a... crime, it begins to take you over. That's why we ensure that a person is of age so they've had time to live and learn to protect themselves. Since a wolf shifter comes into their own at sixteen, we give them two years to see if any signs change. We have to kill them by eighteen before their magic shows. No one in my pack has killed before. We only do it when absolutely necessary."

"So what are you going to do?" The cold wind hit my skin. It was as if my insides were cooling the area around me.

"I'm going to protect you until my last breath." His eyes glowed as he made his vow to me. "I will turn on my family to ensure you stay alive, and we'll bring them to their knees until they are no longer a threat."

My heart grew warm, but the cold void that always seemed to be inside me stayed that way. Maybe that was why I had a hard time fitting in. But I wasn't sure how I felt. I'd just found out that I was up against an ancient secret society that my fated mate was part of and that I was part witch. But we had to focus on the first thing in front of us now—surviving dinner with his brother.

CHAPTER SEVENTEEN

Six o'clock was coming way too fast. I was dreading this dinner, so of course, the hours flew by like minutes.

"So ... you're telling me that Aidan's brother wants to eat dinner with us?" Beth dug through her closet for something to wear.

"He's trying to figure out why I haven't come home yet." Aidan sat on my bed, staring out the window. He'd been a huge mess of tense nerves since his brother had shown up. "After seeing me with the girl I'm supposed to be scoping out and seeing her talking with a couple of witches, he's now doing his own investigation."

"This is still hard to believe." Beth threw a black, short-sleeve shirt on the bed along with a black skirt and fishnet tights. "It sounds like something out of a movie. You're half-witch and destined to rule over everyone. I mean it's badass, but let's hope it's just a story."

"No, not everyone." I loved how she always took things to extremes. "And I mean, I don't see how it could be real. Other than my wolf, I don't feel like I have magic flowing through my veins."

Aidan glanced at me and winced. "An event will cause it."

"What kind of event?" Beth grabbed her clothes from the bed and headed to the door.

"We aren't sure." Aidan shrugged. "No one has ever gotten that far."

A shiver racked my body. I wanted to freak out. My entire identity had changed. I'd always thought I felt different because I was adopted, but learning I was a witch still seemed surreal. What did that mean? And what would happen when my powers awakened? Would I still be me? Anxiety coursed through me, but I couldn't allow it to control me—at least, not until this whole thing with Bradley was done.

"I'll be right back." Beth opened the door and stepped through. "Going to change."

"Okay," I said right before the door shut.

"We shouldn't go." Aidan took my hand in his. "I don't know what he'll do."

"If we don't go, we might make things worse." He appeared suspicious since he'd caught us talking amicably to the witches and learning that the person Aidan was supposed to be tracking was his mate, so there wasn't much of a choice here. "Did he ever tell you where to meet?"

"Yeah," Aidan said with a strained voice. "The Mexican restaurant we went to yesterday."

"Great, but hopefully Jacob and his teammates won't be there this time." I hoped the staff there wouldn't recognize us.

"Considering the amount of sleep Jacob will need to nurse that hangover, I think we're safe." A soft expression crossed his face. He pressed his lips briefly to mine and then brushed his fingertips against my cheek. "I don't want anything to happen to you."

"If what you say is true, then this is only the beginning. Or maybe this is just a fairy tale." It seemed unlikely because of the star birthmark behind my left ear. That detail was oddly specific, but maybe the story was meant to control women.

"That's what I've been hoping for every day since the night I saw your mark." He touched his forehead to mine. "And that the only thing we'll have to fight for is convincing one of our packs to accept us."

"I don't think it would be that easy even if it was only the latter." Jacob had made it clear that he didn't want Aidan in our pack, and Aidan's brother was only humoring us to get close to me.

"You're right there." He stood in a fighter's stance like we were going to war. "It's a damn good thing you're worth fighting for."

It felt like we hadn't been apart for years. "You're not too bad yourself."

He beamed at my words and kissed my lips once more, deepening it and leaving me breathless.

A loud, impatient knock sounded on the door, and Beth called out, "I'm coming in. Break apart."

I pulled back and licked my lips, enjoying the lingering taste.

Beth came in, shaking her head. "I could smell you all the way out there." She slammed the door and rolled her eyes. "I'm glad you gave me a warning, at least."

"Are you about ready?" I picked up my phone from the bed and glanced at the time. "It's five-thirty, so we should head out."

"Some of us need to work at looking presentable." She

motioned to me. "Not everyone can pull off the shirt-and-jeans like you can, but I'm not jealous."

"Oh, whatever." She was gorgeous, and her blue hair emphasized her blue eyes. "You only like to add a dramatic flair to your look."

She moved her head from side to side. "You might be right. Nonetheless ..." She squinted at me and grabbed a darker red lipstick. "Let me put this on, and we're ready to go. My eye makeup from this morning still works."

I stood, lifted my arms over my head, and stretched. Everything I'd learned only hours ago rushed through my brain, but now wasn't the time to freak out.

"All right, let's go." Beth set her lipstick on the table and faced me. "You'd better be glad I love you. Going to dinner with a narrow-minded asswipe is not my idea of fun."

"A little buffer would be great, and having my best friend by my side will make me feel a little better." Having the two people I trusted most in the world with me was the only thing making this manageable.

"You better be glad you added that last part, or my happy ass would be staying here." She placed a hand on her hip and then went for the door. "Let's go. I'm hungry."

I wished I shared her enthusiasm. I couldn't shake the sensation of impending doom. My gut told me that this dinner was going to change the course of my life. Given how I felt, I'd be astonished if I could even eat chips.

"Hey," Aidan said as he took my hand and gently squeezed it. "Everything will be okay. Your hair is down, so he won't be able to see your mark, and Beth won't say a word. And the most important thing is"—he wrapped an arm around my waist—"I won't let anything bad happen to you."

The words were nice, but that was a promise he couldn't keep.

"Stop being Romeo," Beth called from the hallway.

I kissed him and tugged on his arm. "Let's get this over with."

"Gladly."

The three of us walked out of the dorm and climbed into Aidan's Jeep. We rode in silence as if we all dreaded our destination.

"Thank you for coming with us." It really meant a lot. She was putting her neck on the line, but it was nice to have another person there to take the focus off Aidan and me.

"No problem. That's what friends are for." She patted my shoulder comfortingly from the backseat.

We pulled into the parking lot and found another Jeep similar to Aidan's but with Tennessee tags.

I pointed at the red vehicle. "I take it that's him."

"Yeah, of course he would beat us here." Aidan sighed and opened his door.

We climbed out of the car and headed toward the entrance.

"Why is that such a big deal?" Beth glanced around as if she expected him to pop up magically.

"He wants to be in full control. Where the table is located. Where he sits in relation to the three of us. He probably already has our drinks ordered." Aidan opened the front door and motioned for us to enter. "Let's keep Emma as far away from him as we can."

"On it." Beth nodded as we entered.

The hostess was the same as yesterday, and when she saw us, she pressed her hand against her stomach and remained silent.

"Uh ... we're here to meet someone?" If we kept

gawking at each other, things would turn awkward. Better to divert her attention elsewhere.

"Is it the man from yesterday?" Her nose wrinkled in disgust. "Because he's not here."

"No, it's my brother." Aidan placed a hand in his pocket. "He looks similar to me. His car is out there so he should be seated somewhere."

"He's this way." She motioned to her right, and we headed down that hallway.

We entered the bar area, which had open seats around the bar and several high-top tables for four. Bradley was sitting in the far corner, sipping a beer.

"Thank you." I smiled at her and headed to the table.

I took the seat diagonal from Bradley, Beth sat next to me, while Aidan sat across from me, next to his brother.

Bradley's gaze locked on me. "Hello there, Emma."

"Hi, Bradley." I lifted my chin, hoping to look confident, and pointed to my left. "This is Beth, my roommate."

"Ah ... hi." He turned his head to look at his brother. "I'm surprised you're sitting by me and not next to your *girl*."

Great, this started out with a bang.

"Beth doesn't know you, so I thought she'd feel more comfortable sitting next to Emma."

Aidan frowned at him but didn't avert his gaze.

"Isn't it nice that you turned out so *considerate*?" Bradley said the last word with disdain.

"Were you able to connect with the pack?" I wanted to keep this as civil as possible.

"Women shouldn't worry themselves with pack business." Bradley's eyes cut to me. "And frankly, it's none of your business whether I did."

Okay, he had at least come off somewhat cordial earlier.

"Wow, and I thought the men in my pack were bad back at home." Beth stiffened, and her voice rose. "But apparently, more sexist men do exist in the world."

"Obviously, your pack didn't teach their women to keep their mouths shut unless spoken to," Bradley growled and tugged on the sleeve of his shirt.

"What the hell is your problem?" Aidan crossed his arms and scowled. "You aren't here to eat with us, so please enlighten us as to why we're here."

"Well, my meeting was very interesting." He leaned back in his chair and crossed his arms. "Not only is Emma your girl, but she's your fated mate."

"I already told you that." Aidan's voice took on a deep tone.

"Oh, I know." His eyes narrowed. "But you actually met her six years ago and vanished from her life."

"And your point?" Aidan whispered.

A warning coursed down my spine. How did he know all of that?

"At fourteen, you knew she was your fated mate." He glared at his brother in a dare. "So why would you break contact with her?"

"Because I knew you and Dad would never agree to her joining our pack and would refuse to allow me to leave ours," Aidan said slowly.

And he walked right into his brother's trap.

"And you think that changes now?" Bradley grabbed his dark beer and took a long sip.

"Yeah, it does." Aidan grew tense.

"Fuck it." Beth grabbed a tortilla chip and dipped it into salsa. "I'm starving."

Bradley pretended she wasn't even there. "How so?"

"Because you sent me here, and I found her again." His

breathing increased, and his eyes glowed. "I can't give her up a second time."

"So, this is what's become of us?" He set his glass back on the table and shook his head.

"You should be glad I found my fated." Aidan's eyes flicked to mine before focusing back on his brother.

I had no clue what he was trying to tell me, and Beth was focused on her chips, so she wouldn't be any help.

"Under normal circumstances, I would be." Bradley's muddy-gold stare turned to me. "But I remember a question you asked me four years ago."

Aidan became deathly quiet.

"Oh, that's no fun." Bradley lifted his drink and pointed it to me. "Emma, wouldn't you like to know the question he asked?"

"It's irrelevant," Aidan growled.

"I wasn't talking to you." Bradley sneered at me. "Don't you want to know?"

Beth stopped eating and leaned back in her seat. "Well, I'm assuming by her not responding that her answer is 'no.'"

Bradley's large hand slammed on the table, causing his drink to spill and chips to fall from the basket. "Someone ask me the damn question now."

Just like the night before, the people seated near us turned to our table for a second.

The four of us remained quiet until they'd returned to their conversations. Someone would have to ask this before he showed his ass even more.

"Stop making a scene." Aidan grabbed his brother's arm and lowered his voice. "There are humans around."

"No one is going to ask, so if you want to tell us something, you'll have to come right out with it," I said. This guy had to realize we weren't going to play by his rules.

"It'll be nice to put you in your place," Bradley said, the threat clear. "I found him one night, coming back from the border when he was fourteen. I asked him where he'd been, and he said running and thinking." Even though he was talking about his brother, he focused all his attention on me. "He asked me: What would I do if I found my fated mate but she was marked as the cursed one?"

Shit, he knew. There was no going back.

"I told him I would stay away until she turned eighteen, and then I'd kill her with my bare hands." Bradley lifted his hands in his hair. "I asked him why he would ask something so stupid. The right answer was plain as day. He told me no reason."

Beth laughed way too loudly. "Well, he must have had a vivid imagination."

"You see, I think there was a reason." Bradley picked up his drink and downed the rest in one gulp. "So, mind showing me behind your left ear?"

"You're way out of line." Aidan stood and stomped a few steps in the direction of the door. "Come on, let's go." He walked over, took my hand, and pulled me from my seat.

"Why can't she show me, Brother?" Bradley's jaw clenched, disappointment clear on his face. "If you have nothing to hide, it should be a simple request."

"Let's go, Emma," he said and tugged me toward the door.

Beth climbed from her seat and jerked her finger at the alpha heir. "You're an asshole."

"That's a compliment coming from someone like you. Do you realize how embarrassing it was to learn about this from another freshman from another pack? Prescott did what you couldn't." Bradley spoke slowly, and his jaw tightened.

I stopped in my tracks. Shit, Prescott was Jacob's roommate and part of the society.

"Why am I not surprised?" Aidan muttered and stepped toward the entrance.

Bradley rubbed at his forearms. "Oh, and Aidan, if you leave, you'll be a traitor."

"If that's what it means, then so be it." Aidan turned his back on his brother and went to the door.

"Don't worry, Emma. We'll find you." A sick chuckle filled my ears as we left the restaurant.

He knew it wouldn't be long before God knew how many would know. We had no choice but to go visit the witches to see if there was any way they could help us.

CHAPTER EIGHTEEN

Thankfully, the Civic and truck were in the driveway of the witches' house. I'd been paranoid that we'd been followed, but it appeared we were in the clear.

"Are we sure this is smart?" Aidan's voice held trepidation. "Witches are known to be violent and hold grudges."

"All species are known for that," Beth grumbled in the backseat. "I mean, look at your pack, for God's sake. You hold a grudge against an entire gender. What does that say about you?"

She had a point there. I felt a connection with each witch. "Look, they are nice. Well, Finn is a little cold, but the others are warm and open."

"So, maybe we should be leery of Finn." Aidan glanced at me. "I don't want to risk you getting hurt or worse."

"There is a difference between being standoffish and having something bad happen to you." Aidan might have grown up with hatred in his heart, but it was clear he'd been raised with his family. Amethyst had let me in on the fact that Finn had been adopted. No one could understand growing up different or scarred unless they lived it.

"I don't know ..." he started.

"We have no other options. Your brother just declared war on us." We had to do something. "Should we just sit around and wait for them to kill me?" I'd been doing okay until this point, but now all of the feelings were crashing down on me.

"Of course not." He nibbled on his lip. "Let's run."

"Where?" He was upset and not thinking rationally. Granted, I could say the same about myself right now. "If the curse is true, then I'm half-witch. I'll need witches to help me."

He paused.

"I don't think he thought that part through." Beth opened the Jeep door and began to climb out. "Just in case it isn't clear, I'm on Emma's side." She shut the door and ran up to the front porch.

"Hey, it'll be okay." I took his hand. "I promise I don't have a death wish. I think this is the most logical first step. Then, we can run like you suggested."

"Okay, but know it won't take them long to mobilize." Aidan turned off the car and scratched the back of his neck. "So we can't take long. We'll need to get away from here fast. That's why I don't see the point."

The front door opened, and after Beth entered, Samuel stepped out, tapping his foot as he waited for us.

"Come on." It's not like we could leave Beth behind. Bradley knew she was with us, so she was stuck with us. I hadn't even considered that until now.

I got out of the car with Aidan following my lead.

"What's going on?" Samuel frowned when his eyes landed on Aidan.

"We've got a problem, and we're hoping you can give us guidance." Or a place to start.

"My initial advice is to leave that elitist behind," Finn said as he stepped out of the house and glared at Aidan.

I should've expected this. "No, he's not here to be confrontational."

"Says you." Finn rubbed his hands together. "He looks as uncomfortable here as he should."

"Look, Emma trusts you." Aidan straightened his shoulders and grimaced. "So I'm here for her."

"One comment we don't like, and you're out." Samuel held up a finger in emphasis. "All it'll take is one time."

"Fine." Aidan nodded.

"Man, that's too easy. His kind is a danger to us all," Finn said through his teeth.

"Hey, I'm a shifter too." I couldn't help but point out his hypocrisy.

"But you don't hate witches or try to kill as many as possible." Finn's hands clenched into fists as if he were coming unglued.

"Look, we won't be here long." Maybe Aidan was right and this had been a horrible decision. I hadn't expected Finn to be so adamantly against him.

"Fine." He moved out of the doorway so Aidan and I could pass.

I stepped into the living room and found Coral and Amethyst sitting on the couch with Beth.

Amethyst's body tensed when she saw me. "What's wrong?"

Sometimes, it was freaky how much she could gather within seconds of someone entering a room. I barely had a chance to get my bearings. "There's something I need your guidance on."

"What is it?" Coral shifted in her seat as her attention flicked to Aidan. "Does it have to do with him?"

Yeah, there was no love lost between them and Aidan. "No ... yes ... kind of." That probably didn't help things.

Samuel and Finn walked around us and stood facing Aidan and me.

Beth lifted a hand toward me. "Just come out with it."

"It's not as easy as just coming out with it." I was getting annoyed with her, but it wasn't right. I was projecting things onto her. "I found out something about myself that's hard to believe."

Coral crossed her legs and turned toward me. "That you're part witch?"

"Well, that's part of it, yes." That was fucking unsettling. "How the hell did you know?"

"It's part of being a witch." Amethyst placed her elbows on her knees. "The first time you touch, it alerts witches that you're one of us and what coven you belong to."

"I didn't feel anything when we touched." This could be problematic. How many people knew I was a witch?

"You probably didn't know what to look for." Amethyst straightened and dropped her hands in her lap. "Hell, I even mentioned it when we met. You had no clue?"

"No, none." I began to doubt everything I knew. People knew me better than I knew my damn self. "Wait ... I'm part of a coven? Why didn't you tell me?"

"It would appear so." Samuel looked sheepish and shrugged. "And a descendant of ours, though we are just getting to know you. We thought maybe you weren't ready to tell us. I mean witches aren't supposed to be able to reproduce with shifters."

"That's one reason we were so accepting of you." Finn's chin jutted, and he tapped his foot on the ground. "Even though you're half-shifter."

"Don't listen to him." Coral waved him off. "Amethyst

knew you and Beth were not a threat because there has never been animosity flowing from you two toward us, unlike your mate there."

Amethyst looked at Aidan with concern. "He's scared now. There isn't any hate."

"That makes him even more dangerous." Finn took a menacing step toward Aidan. "What do wolves do when they're afraid?"

"Stop it," I said as I turned around to face Finn. "He's my fated mate, so he can't hate witches or he'd be hating half of me."

"That's a good point." Samuel dropped his arms. All sense of tension was erased as if magic had filled my words.

"Don't be a dumbass," Finn grumbled.

"Look, apparently I'm the cursed one, and there is a large number of wolf shifters banding together to kill me." There went easing them into the conversation.

Beth smacked her leg. "You don't do anything half-heartedly, do you?"

Coral tapped her chin. "Wait ... why do they want to kill you?"

"Aidan, want to fill them in?" I wanted someone else to take over.

"My family is part of The Hallowed Guild, and a half-witch, half-wolf shifter bearing the mark has been deemed a risk to our kind, and she must be exterminated before she comes into her powers." Aidan touched my shoulder. "Was that blunt enough?"

"Yes, subtlety is not a strong suit for either of you, but in all fairness, we don't have time to be political." Beth ran a hand through her hair.

"Wait ... The Hallowed Guild?" Amethyst said slowly,

her eyes going to the window. "The very society that's known for killing witches?"

"They aren't supposed to unless they're marked." Aidan sighed. "Look, I may have been trained as a member of the society, but I've been trying to get answers on how to protect her." His eyes were full of love and determination. "I've turned my back on my family and pack for her. I'm not sure how else I can prove that I'm all-in."

"They do a lot more than kill marked witches." Finn scowled at him. "So I'm sorry if I'm not jumping up and down to trust you."

"Just shut it down for a second, Finn." Amethyst's voice was cold and very uncharacteristic of her. She stood and headed straight to me. "Are you marked?"

"Uh ... yeah." I was a little uncomfortable with the look in her eye as she approached me. "Or we wouldn't be having this conversation."

"Can I see it?" She scanned me like she was expecting it to be obvious.

"Yeah, okay." I had grown self-conscious about the mark given how everyone reacted when they saw it. Now I knew the perfectly shaped star was there for a very specific reason. I moved my hair aside and turned so she could see behind my ear.

"Holy shit." Her small, warm fingers traced the edges of the star. "It's the pentagram."

"Wait... that isn't possible." Finn stepped over next to her and blinked a few times. He gasped as he took in the mark. "How the hell?"

"Does the star mean something to you?" Aidan's jaw clenched, and he turned around to glance out the window. "We need to get moving before they track us. It's essential to be as far away from here as possible."

He was right. "Can you help us?"

"Hell yeah, we can." Samuel headed to the stairs. "Let me grab some things, and we'll move out."

"No, I don't want to disrupt your lives." I'd only hoped for some insight. I hadn't meant for them to come with us.

"You don't understand." Amethyst's usual warm demeanor slid back into place. "It's our honor to help. We've been waiting for you."

There was another damn thing I didn't know. I didn't feel like I was even the same person. "What do you mean?"

Amethyst touched my arm as if to offer me support. "Do you remember my comment about the witches one day having an all-women council?"

"Please don't say it involves me." I didn't think I could take on anything else.

"Well, then, this conversation is about to get awkward really quickly." Coral looked at Beth. "I'll go pack some things. You two better hurry and get your stuff. We need to be on the road in twenty minutes."

"Wait... what's the plan?" I felt bad. It was like I'd uprooted six other lives in the span of a few hours.

"We're taking you to our coven." Finn narrowed his eyes. "Maybe he should stay behind."

Aidan growled.

"If he doesn't come, neither do I." He was the most important person to me. There was no way I could get through this without him. Okay, that wasn't true. The truth was I didn't want to do it without him.

"Of course." Finn huffed and lowered his head. "Be glad we need you." He turned his back toward me and went up the stairs.

"Let's roll." Beth stood and made her way to the door.

"If Bradley acted that poorly in the restaurant, there's no way in hell I want to see him completely unhinged."

"Yeah, he tends to act without thinking." Aidan's jaw clenched. "Let's go. We can run by a store to get more clothes and toiletries tomorrow."

Coral gave him a thumbs up. "That sounds good. There is a Walmart close by that we can take you to. Go ahead and get in the car." Coral called over her shoulder. "We won't be long."

Beth, Aidan, and I rushed out the door. We had to get out of here before we got caught.

Aidan

IT WAS HARD BEING around the three witches though they were nice. However, Finn brought out the worst in me. The only reason I behaved was because my mate liked and trusted them.

I'd been raised to hate them. It was hammered into our heads how evil they were. They represented overvalued women who seduced males with their feminine wiles. But they also said the same thing about Emma, and it wasn't even close to the truth.

For her, I would have to trust them, and if it went south, I'd fight like hell to protect her.

Emma

Two hours later, we were pulling onto another backroad in what could only be described as the boondocks.

"At least, we can go for a run." Beth yawned in the backseat. "It's been forever since I've shifted."

Ever since we'd started college over a month ago, I hadn't shifted either. My wolf was getting restless, too. "Let's get settled in first."

Luckily, we'd left campus without any issues, and surprisingly, it had been smooth sailing. I was waiting for the other shoe to drop.

Finn and Samuel were leading in the truck, and Coral and Amethyst were behind us. We were in the middle to ensure we didn't get lost.

"I've lost my damn mind." Aidan squeezed the steering wheel so hard his knuckles turned white. "I'm going to a fucking coven."

It took effort to hold my laughter in. "But you're learning that there is more to this than you realized."

"And I'm not sure I buy it." He huffed. "I mean, why would the witches be involved?"

"You do remember it was a witch who supposedly cursed your alpha." Beth leaned in between the two seats, and her hair looked almost black in the darkness. "So... I mean... does it really not make sense to you?"

"She's right, you know." This was bigger than Aidan even realized, and the fact was weighing heavy on me.

"Yeah, yeah." He looked at me. "You better be damn glad I love you."

My heart skipped a beat. That was the second time he'd said it. Maybe it hadn't been an accident the first time. "You better be glad I love you too and put up with your broodiness."

I tried hiding the smile but couldn't. "You love me, huh?"

"Oh, dear God." Beth fell back in her seat. "Do I need to be here for this?"

"You decided to ride with us." I stuck my tongue out at her. "You could've ridden with Amethyst and Coral."

"Because I wanted to stay close with my bestie." She pointed at me. "I didn't realize I'd have to listen to verbal-foreplay."

I burst out laughing. I needed that. "Really? That's what you call it?"

"You guys are totally going to get it on tonight. You have no more secrets, and you're saying I love you. Just make sure I don't hear anything. There's no telling how we'll be set up over there."

"I promise you'll survive."

The guys turned down a gravel road that finally seemed to be leading somewhere. As Aidan followed, the car jarred over the pebbles. The woods were thick, and after another mile, an expansive subdivision appeared. The fifty or so houses were modest but very well kept, and they looked to be around twenty years old.

As we drove through the neighborhood, I saw that a large grassy knoll occupied the center of the area. There had to be at least a hundred people standing there, facing our vehicle.

Samuel parked alongside the perimeter, and we pulled in right behind him.

"I hope we don't regret this," Aidan mumbled. "There is no way we'll make it out of here alive if they turn on us."

I had to trust my gut. "We'll be fine." I opened the car door. It was time to figure out the whole truth about why I was here and what they expected from me.

CHAPTER NINETEEN

When I stepped out of the car, I could feel the witches' eyes on me. Hoping I was overreacting, I glanced in their direction and wound up catching one set of eyes.

"Don't be nervous." Amethyst walked over to me. "Allowing you to stay is a coven decision, so all witches are present."

"I'm not sure that's comforting," Beth grumbled and slammed her door.

"It's fine." Amethyst waved her off with a giggle. "Come on." She took my arm and pulled me toward the grassy area.

As I passed Aidan, he snagged my hand.

"Do not go anywhere without me," Aidan said quietly so only I could hear him. His body was tense like he was prepared for an attack any second.

Finn stood off to the side as Samuel ran to an older lady who looked strikingly similar. She had to be his mother.

"I guess we're taking up the rear," Coral said from behind us as she caught up with Beth.

"It appears that way." Beth chuckled. "But I'm okay with it."

The woman standing front and center nodded, causing pieces of long, blonde hair to fall over her shoulders. She was about Amethyst's height, and her eyes were a pale purple.

She pulled Amethyst into a tight hug. "It's good to see you, but what was the emergency?"

It was close to ten at night on a weekday, so it probably seemed random that we'd come here so late.

"Mom, she's the girl." Amethyst pointed at me.

Of course, this would be her mother.

"The girl?" Her mom asked the words slowly and scanned me from head to toe.

"She has the pentagram mark." Amethyst motioned to the other witches who were near enough to hear.

"But she reeks of shifter." The witch closest to the lady wrinkled her nose at me. Her long, carrot-colored hair and freckles made her expression that much more disgusted.

"Because she's a hybrid." Coral's tone was impatient, and she gestured to my ear. "Emma, show them the mark."

I was prepared to ask if I should sit and beg too. If this was what it took for them to help me, it was a small price to pay. I moved my hair to one side of my neck and turned so the witches could see.

"Dear Goddess." Amethyst's mom placed a hand on her chest. "It's true."

Murmurs came from behind her, and Aidan tensed even more. I wasn't quite sure how that was possible.

"Then there is only one answer." Amethyst's mom nodded at me. "You are allowed to stay with us."

I warned them to make sure they understood what they

were risking. They couldn't go into this blind. "Look, there is a group of shifters who want to kill me."

"You act as if that is out of the ordinary, but it doesn't matter. You're one of us and marked," a woman who was a few people back called out. "We protect our own."

The other witches mumbled their agreement and then began making their way back to the houses.

Okay, I hadn't expected that. "Uh... where are they going?"

"The decision has been made." Amethyst's mom held out her hand to me. "I'm Beatrice."

"I'm Emma and this"—I nodded at Aidan—"is my fated mate, Aidan, and then my best friend, Beth."

"I don't get anything but wolf shifters off the two of you," the carrot-haired woman stated as she pulled Coral into her arms.

"They aren't hybrids." Coral hugged her back. "Guys, this is my mom, Rowan."

Now that she'd mentioned it, I could see similarities. "Hi."

"And this is my mom." Samuel dragged his mom over.

Her eyes were the same sage color, but her hair was a dark brown. She was the shortest among us, and there was a kindness to her. "My name is Sage. It's an honor to meet you." She bowed her head.

Yeah, no. That wouldn't work. Right now, I wanted time alone so I could scream, cry, fall apart, or something equally dramatic. I wasn't sure how much longer I could keep myself together. "Look, it's been a long day."

"Of course, dear." Beatrice's kind words were soothing. "Let's get you all settled in, and we can reconvene in the morning."

"That's probably best." Aidan's shoulders relaxed ever

so slightly. "She's been through a lot in the last twenty-four hours."

"I can only imagine." Rowan squeezed Beth's shoulder with a thoughtful expression. "Would you like to stay with Coral and me?"

"Sure." Beth appeared beside me. "Is that okay with you two?"

"Of course." She didn't need our permission. I trusted Coral, so it wasn't a huge deal.

"Then, Aidan and Emma can stay with me." Beatrice motioned to the house right across from us in the middle of the neighborhood.

"I'm staying in the same room with her," Aidan said matter-of-factly, not to be argued with. "I can't leave her side with what's going on."

"I didn't expect you to." Beatrice patted his arm and reassured him. "We have an extra bedroom with a queen-sized bed. You two should be able to manage."

My body heated. We'd be sleeping together. Under normal circumstances, I'd have been thrilled, especially since this would be our first time, but I was exhausted.

"Yeah, we will." Aidan squeezed my hand gently.

"All right, Rowan and Sage, you all come over in the morning, and we can talk over breakfast." Beatrice waved at us to follow. "We can figure everything out then."

Aidan and I followed behind her.

"Hey, wait up," Amethyst called out and walked beside me.

"I have some clothes you can wear until we can get you some of your own." Amethyst cleared her throat and shrugged uncomfortably. "Sorry, Aidan, you're out of luck."

"I'll be fine." Aidan scanned our surroundings, looking

for any threats or for anything that could go awry at any second.

"Night guys," Samuel called out as he, Sage, and Finn headed toward a house together.

"Are Finn and Samuel related?" I'd never gotten that vibe from them before, but Amethyst had mentioned that he was adopted. I'd assumed it was by a family member.

"No, but Finn has lived with them since he was a baby." Sadness filled Beatrice's words.

"Not with his parents?" Maybe I was getting the final piece of the puzzle.

"His parents died a year or so after he was born." Amethyst's shoulders sagged, and she rubbed her hands together. "They died protecting his aunt, his mother's sister."

"From what?" That was horrible. Who could've done something so horrible?

"Wolves," Beatrice said painfully.

No wonder he hated wolves. I couldn't blame him. "What do you mean?"

"We'll talk in the morning." Beatrice opened the front door and held it for us. "Your room is up the stairs and to the left."

As we walked in, the smell of rosemary and basil hit my nose. The house had gray walls, and the floor was hardwood. A large brown couch sat in front of a flat-screen television with a rocking chair to the side. The stairs were in the middle of the far living room wall, so I headed in that direction.

"I'll take you." Amethyst stepped in front of us. "Mine is right across from yours, but don't worry; we each have our own bathroom." She climbed the stairs, expecting us to follow.

"Thank you for letting us stay here." It meant a lot to me that a perfect stranger was willing to take us in.

"Of course." Beatrice crossed the living room to a doorway on the right that appeared to lead into the kitchen or down a hall. "Now, get some rest. You need it after the day you've had."

"Come on, Angel." Aidan brushed my arm with his hand.

This time, the pet name warmed my heart.

At the top of the stairs, I stopped.

Amethyst opened the door on the left. "Here you two are. Home sweet home." She entered the room and turned on the lights.

It was smaller than my room back at home but more spacious than the dorm. The queen bed took up most of the area, but there was enough room for a chest of drawers with a television on top. The room was the standard light gray with light-colored, shaggy carpet. The bedsheets were an earthy brown, which fit the house perfectly.

"This is great." I let go of Aidan's hand and gave her a small hug. "Thank you."

"Of course." She held up a finger. "Let me go grab you some clothes."

"You don't have to." I hated to be a bother.

"No, it's fine. They may be short on you, but it'll be more comfortable." She ran out of the room, leaving Aidan and me alone.

"Are you okay?" Aidan asked quietly. He stared deep into my eyes as if daring me to lie.

"Does it matter?" I hadn't chosen the cards life had dealt me. Never would I have chosen this path.

"Of course it does." He stepped into my bubble and

placed his fingers underneath my chin, gently forcing my head up to prevent me from averting my eyes.

He knew all my tricks.

"But it doesn't." I felt powerless. "Me not being okay doesn't change the situation we're in." My heart picked up its pace. "Not only has my life changed, but I've put you, Beth, and this whole coven at risk. Do you know what it feels like to have that on your conscience?" Maybe I needed to run away and save them all.

"Emma," he growled in warning.

"Here you go." Amethyst entered the room and handed me a set of matching frilly pajamas. "And just know I'll be casting a perimeter spell tonight, so if you sneak out, I'll know."

Her gift was really inconvenient. "You wouldn't."

"The fact she even had to say that isn't funny at all." Aidan wore an unreadable expression on his face. "You do realize if you ran, I'd find you."

Oh, dear God. I had both of them on my case now. "I'm not running away." I took the clothes off the bed and found the doorway into the bathroom, stepped inside, and shut the door, not bothering to turn the lights on.

My wolf surged forward until I could see without a problem in the dark. There was a plastic tub in the corner of the room and a toilet between it and the wall. The counters had his-and-her sinks.

"She'll be okay," Amethyst whispered as if she thought I couldn't hear her.

He remained silent.

I quickly changed and walked back out. "See, I'm wearing the pink nightclothes. You can rest easy now."

"Okay, then." Amethyst stepped out of the room, feeling uncomfortable. "Goodnight."

Once she'd shut the door, I climbed into the bed and lay facing the window. The moon was high in the cloudless sky, but even my wolf wasn't yearning to get out. It felt as if she was as confused as I was, which didn't make any sense.

"Hey." Aidan's voice was low, and I heard him remove his shirt and pants before climbing into bed with me. He placed his arm under my neck and wrapped his other arm around my body, pulling me against his chest.

My skin buzzed, our bond springing to life. I closed my eyes, relishing the feeling and trying to focus on it while blocking everything else out.

He lifted his hand from my waist and trailed his fingertips along my arm. His touches fueled the friction running through me.

I turned over, desperate for his kiss. I needed him. My lips claimed his, and he hesitated for a moment before kissing me back.

His taste filled me, and his hands sliding up my body heated me in more ways than one. I deepened our kiss, needing him to stimulate me in all ways. My hands touched his naked chest, flaming my arousal. The feel of his skin right against mine made me dizzy.

I moaned and tried to get closer to him.

His hand tangled in my hair as he hardened against me. He removed his lips from mine. "You're making me crazy."

"Good." The fact that I affected him turned me on even more. I lowered my hands to the waist of his boxers. Right before I was ready to slip them inside, he grabbed my hand and stilled them.

"No." He pulled back and stared directly into my eyes. "We're not doing that."

"What?" Tears burned my eyes. "But I thought..."

"Not like this." Aidan let my hand go and wrapped his

arm around me. "Not when you're trying not to think about something."

"But I want you." That was plain and simple. "I've always wanted you."

"And I've always wanted you." He brushed his lips against mine. "We've waited this long. One more night won't hurt. When I claim you, I want it to be for us only. Right now, you're confused and close to a breakdown. You deserve better than that."

He made sense, and now the only thing I felt was shame. "I'm sorry. I do want you."

"I know you do." He gave me a small smile. "And you will be mine in every way that counts. Just, not tonight, okay? We can kiss, we can talk, or we can just lie here and cuddle. I'm all yours and not going anywhere. You waited for me. Now it's my turn to wait for you."

"I guess I can make it through one more night." I kissed him one last time.

"We'll figure things out tomorrow. I promise," he said as he pulled me into his arms again. "Right now, you need rest."

He was right. My heart and soul were tired. "Okay."

I closed my eyes, enjoying the buzz of our connection, and drifted to sleep, hoping he'd be able to keep that promise.

Aidan

NEVER IN A MILLION years would I expect to be sleeping under the same roof as witches; let alone surrounded by a coven. Everything inside me screamed for me to run, but I had to get over that. This woman in my arms would now, and always, be my number one priority. If she was part witch, then they couldn't all be bad. Emma was the more sincere and pure person I'd ever met.

Dad had to be wrong, and I would do whatever it took to protect the woman I loved including her friends. I'd risk everything for her to never be hurt again... even if it meant fighting against my own pack.

CHAPTER TWENTY

The sound of the front door opening woke me. The buzzing of my skin was still strong, and I raised my head from a hard, sexy chest.

"Hey there, sleepyhead." Aidan's voice was deep with sleep, and a huge smile spread across his face.

"Hey, you." I leaned toward him and brushed my lips against his.

"Uh... no," he murmured and raised up to capture my lips again.

"Nope, not happening." I pulled out of his arms and jumped to my feet. "Morning breath. Let's wait until we get toothbrushes."

"I don't give a damn," he growled. "Get your hot ass back here."

"Nuh-uh." I tried to hide my smile and pointed at him as I nudged the bathroom door wider with my hip. "And honestly, you should brush your teeth, too."

"You stinker." He jumped out of bed and charged me.

A loud laugh escaped me as he hoisted me into his arms

and planted a huge kiss on my lips. He pinned me to the door and deepened the kiss.

It wasn't fair. How could I deny him? I melted into his embrace and kissed him back. Right when I began getting dizzy, he pulled back with a smug-ass grin.

"See, no brushing needed or required." His breath hit my face, and it somehow still smelled minty.

How was that even possible?

"No, I think you learned your lesson." I bet my breath was rancid. Served him right.

A loud knock on the bedroom door interrupted us.

"Get your asses out here before you guys make all of us uncomfortable downstairs." Beth's amused voice came through the door. "Don't make me come in there."

That had ruined the mood, so I pulled away. "Let me change back into my clothes before we cause a scene."

"Are you sure?" There was a twinkle in his eye.

I loved seeing him this way. It'd been far too long. "No, but we need to figure out what's going on and learn more about what the witches are expecting from me."

"You're right." He kissed me quickly once more. "Let's get moving."

Minutes later, we entered the kitchen to find a full table.

The kitchen was large, and the rectangular table seated twelve. The wooden table matched the cabinets, and everyone was piling their plates full of eggs, bacon, and toast.

Beatrice sat at one of the head spots at the table with Sage on one side and Rowan on the other. Samuel sat between his mother and Finn. On the other side of the table, Coral sat next to her mother and Amethyst. Beth, of course, was next to Amethyst, steering clear of Finn.

Not wanting to make him feel unapproachable, I sat beside him with Aidan sitting on my other side.

Finn's eyes widened a little.

He hadn't expected that. Good. Trying not to act weird, I grabbed my plate and dished some food out for myself. "This looks delicious."

"Beth was so happy when we got here and saw normal food." Coral snorted. "She thought we'd be having frog eyes and blood soup."

"In all the movies, witches never eat normal things." Beth stabbed her eggs with her fork. "I mean, you can't blame me."

"And movies convey shifters as cold-blooded killers." Finn arched an eyebrow, daring her to argue.

She would take the bait.

"So Jacob from *Twilight* is portrayed like that?" Beth chewed with her mouth wide open.

"Did..."

"Enough," Beatrice said loudly, her voice ringing with authority. "We know the media doesn't paint us in the right light. Stop bickering."

Beth glanced at me, and she placed her fork on the table. "I just got mommed."

"Someone has to keep you two in check." Samuel chuckled and took a sip of orange juice. "Besides, we are now on the same side."

Finn frowned at him. "As fucking wolves?"

Sage pointedly looked at Finn. "Yes. Seeing as our future leader is part wolf, I'm thinking we're going to have to come to grips with it."

"This has to be a joke?" He scoffed and bit his lip. "This is supposed to be impossible. What are the chances of two witches getting pregnant by shifters?"

"Two?" Aidan had made it sound like I was the only hybrid.

"We used to live in Mount Juliet." Rowan picked up her cup of coffee. "One of our coven members fell in love with a shifter. When she found out she was pregnant, we were all in shock."

"Mount Juliet?" It couldn't be a coincidence. "That's where we're from."

Rowan stopped mid-sip and put her mug down. She examined me from head to toe. "Could it be possible?"

"Let's not get ahead of ourselves," Beatrice said as she stared me down. "Finn's aunt fell in love with a shifter named Hawk."

"Wait..." Aidan stiffened. "We had a traitor in our pack named Hawk. He was killed for having a relationship with a witch."

"Oh my God." Samuel dropped his fork on the plate.

"Just a relationship?" Beatrice's question hung in the air.

"Well, yeah. It's one of Dad's favorite stories to tell. Apparently, my father caught Hawk hanging out with a witch one night in a secret clearing, so they kept a watch on him." Aidan's eyes crinkled as he recalled the story. "They followed him one night to an abandoned cabin in the woods. He must have realized they were there because, before my father could attack, Hawk came out with his hands in the air. My dad killed him right there."

"He wasn't dead." Rowan's voice was barely above a whisper. "At least, not yet."

"How do you know that?" I wasn't sure how I felt, but I was pretty certain we were figuring out who my parents were.

"I was there." Rowan stared out the window. "Hawk

crawled back to the house to find Winnie dead. She'd died during childbirth as Hawk was attacked. He said we had to get the baby to a pack that would accept her. His pack's enemy bordered their territory. Finn's mother, Wanda, and father, Aldo, told me to leave and alert the coven. The wolves might be coming for us, and we had to go. They asked me to take care of Finn if something were to happen to them. They were going to burn the cabin down with Winnie's body inside so the wolves would never know she'd been pregnant. They were releasing her ashes to Mother Nature."

Her hands shook as she took a moment to collect her thoughts. "You see, Wanda used her energy to keep Hawk from dying until he'd gotten you to them. Aldo cloaked them. I have no clue what happened, but they never returned."

"I was found on the border with a dead wolf beside me." My eyes burned as realization set in. "Your dad killed my father." I turned toward Aidan, trying to process it all. Obviously, it hadn't been his fault, but how he was raised was clear in front of my face. The very man who murdered my father raised my fated mate. No wonder he struggled when he saw my mark.

"I'm sorry." He averted his gaze to the table, and his jaw tensed.

"You don't need to apologize." It wasn't fair of me to make him feel that way. Hell, he'd turned his back on his family for me. When it mattered, he did what was right.

"Yes, he does." Finn's chair fell back as he stood and pointed at Aidan. "Your family killed my parents because they were witches."

"Finn, sit down," Beatrice said loudly, her voice laced with a hint of anger.

"No." He clenched his hands and took a menacing step toward Aidan.

Surprisingly, Aidan didn't react, instead, he waited like he was going to allow Finn to beat him up as punishment. Oh, hell no.

I stood and placed my hands on Finn's shoulders, halting him. "You'd better calm your ass down before I make you," I growled, staring him in the eye. "He's no more responsible for your parents' death than I am. They died protecting my mother."

That gave him pause. "But..."

"There are no damn buts." The alpha will laced my words, taking me completely off guard. That had never happened before.

Even though he was a witch, something flickered in his eyes, and his breathing calmed. "You better be glad you're my family." The last word held emotion, but he tried to rein it in.

He needed time to deal with it. Even I needed more time too.

"And you"—I spun around and glared at my mate—"don't ever act that way again. You walked away from your family to do the right thing. Do not act like you deserve punishment again, or I'll kick your ass."

"Damn." Beth propped her head in her hands and grinned. "This is better than television."

"Think about it." Samuel touched Finn's arm. "She's your family now."

Something passed in Finn's eyes as he took in his words. "You were only found with a wolf?"

"My parents found two witches as they left the perimeter," Aidan said. "They'd uncloaked themselves, thinking they were safe, but my dad had kept his pack on guard, expecting a woman full of anger to come and demand to know what had happened to her lover. They never stood a chance." He rubbed a hand down his face and sighed.

I took his hand in mine. It was odd that the news was hitting him harder than me.

"Okay, enough of this conversation. Let's finish breakfast, and then you all run to Walmart to get what you need for the next several weeks." Beatrice picked up her cup with shaky hands. "Then tonight, we'll induct Emma into our coven since she's rightfully one of us."

"What does that mean?" They would have to treat me like a newbie.

"That each one of the members must accept you." Beatrice nodded. "Nothing more. Our magic and coven don't require sacrifices to join but do prefer the person to be a descendant of our coven."

"Okay." I could do it. It would be nice to have a connection to my mother. I knew all about being a wolf shifter but nothing about being a witch.

"Then, it's settled."

It was around nine p.m. when Amethyst knocked on the door. "Be ready to head out in ten minutes."

"Okay." I put on the new shirt and jeans I'd bought from Walmart and moved closer to Aidan.

Needing a moment with him, I wrapped my arms around his shoulders and stood on my tiptoes to kiss him.

He pulled me tight against his chest.

"Are you okay?" He'd been off for a little while this morning after the revelation about my parents.

"Yeah, I just feel responsible, which is stupid." He

rubbed a hand down his face and dropped them to his sides. "I was just a baby, but I hate that my family did this to all of you."

"And that's what makes you different from them." I cupped his face and looked into his eyes. "You grew up knowing right from wrong. They didn't. In their minds, they were doing the right thing."

He huffed. "I hadn't thought about it that way, but you're right. They think the witches cursed them for no good reason. But he turned his back on his own blood."

"Both sides were wronged." At least the witches, though, were protecting me. The Hallowed Guild wanted me dead for being only half-wolf. "The witches accept me, but it's because they are used to the idea of female leaders. Wolves aren't."

"And fate had just the plan to make sure I fell in line." He gave me a tender smile as he leaned in for a quick kiss.

"That probably helped your case, but it doesn't matter." I grabbed his shirt with both hands. "There is no one else in this entire world I want by my side."

"Well, that's good since I'm not going anywhere." He wrapped his arms around my waist and placed his forehead against mine. "I made that mistake once, and I've regretted it every day."

"It's in the past." I didn't want anything to darken our bond now. "Let's just focus on today and our future."

"I can do that."

"Emma! Aidan! Let's go," Amethyst called from the bottom of the stairs.

"It's time to get initiated." I took his hand and opened the door. We hurried downstairs to meet Beatrice and Amethyst.

As soon as we caught up to them, Beatrice opened the

door, and the four of us filed out. Just like last night, the large group of witches waited in the center grassy field.

We headed over to them, and Beth waved from the road as we passed her.

"Aidan, you should stay here," Amethyst reassured him and touched his arm. "It won't be long, and we'll bring her right back."

He stilled but didn't release my hand.

"It'll be fine." I smiled at him and pecked his lips. "I'll be right back."

"Okay." He nodded, letting go of me.

I followed Amethyst and Beatrice to the middle of the field. The witches fell back as Beatrice took the lead. Sage was on her right, and Rowan was on her left.

"It's not often we find one of us who has been left behind, but last night, we were given a gift from the Goddess herself." Beatrice took my hand and turned to her coven. "Emma is our late Winnie's daughter."

"Our High Priestess?" One of the witches at the front gasped and placed a hand on her chest.

"My mother was the priestess?" I turned to Beatrice, surprised. She hadn't informed me of this.

"Yes, she was. That was one reason why her death impacted us so much. We moved here right after." Beatrice focused back on the coven. "I'm honored to say she is now one of us."

One by one, the witches bowed their heads in acceptance. Energy began coursing around us, and soon it was pooling under my skin. It was similar to my mate bond with Aidan but seemed to pour in from the ground and all around me. It traveled to the dark spot inside me that had always felt like a cold void.

"See, quick and easy." Amethyst beamed as she touched my arm.

A loud howl filled the air, and Beatrice stiffened beside me.

"Mom, what's wrong?" Amethyst's purple eyes seemed brighter somehow.

"Emma!" Aidan yelled as he turned and ran in my direction.

"The perimeter." Beatrice turned, scanning the area where the howl had come from. "They're here."

Holy shit. They'd found us. How the hell was that possible?

CHAPTER TWENTY-ONE

"We need to hide you." Aidan grabbed my hand and began pulling me toward the house.

"No, I can't hide." They were here for me. They would kill as many people as possible to get to me. I couldn't hide like a coward.

"They're here to kill you." Aidan glared at me, and his face creased with worry. "This isn't negotiable."

"I'm glad you agree." I loved him with all my heart and soul, but I wouldn't let him control me.

He sighed with relief.

Oh, bless his heart. I yanked my hand free and ran toward everyone else.

"Emma, what the hell?" Aidan called after me and hurried to catch up. "I said this isn't negotiable."

"I know, but that doesn't mean I agree to your terms." I stopped and turned around, ready to fight him on this. "They are here for me. The witches are protecting me. I can't turn my back on them."

Twenty wolves charged toward us, and I stayed stationary, watching to see if any more appeared.

"Why is there such a small number?" This didn't make any sense.

"They didn't realize we'd be with a coven." Aidan blew out a breath. "So they must have followed us, and this is who we got. This is a good thing."

A wolf lunged at a male witch. The witch held his hands up, and his lips began to move, but the wolf bit into his throat and ripped it out.

Holy shit. The fight had just started, and blood had already been spilled.

"Everybody, we need to ready ourselves!" Beatrice yelled as more witches ran past us. "We need to let them come to us. Our fear shouldn't give them the upper hand."

"You're right, Momma." Amethyst straightened her shoulders and stood next to her mother. "The wolves are petrified. They didn't know what they were running into."

"As of now, we have the advantage. Don't forget that." Everyone needed to realize it. I needed to instill confidence, but there was no telling if more shifters were coming or how many of us would die before we could take them out. "We need to leave one alive to question. We need to know what else to expect."

"You're right." Beatrice nodded at me. "Make sure one stays alive, at least, for a little while."

Beth ran over to me and glanced back at the fight that was breaking out. "Emma, what do we do?"

"I'm going to shift and fight beside the witches." It was the only real solution I had.

"Emma, please." Aidan's eyes were full of fear, and his hands shook as he reached for me. "They're here for you."

"Then let's do this together." If my destiny was to lead, I would start now.

He grimaced and rubbed a hand over his heart. "Fine,

but we stay together."

"Promise." That was an easy vow to make.

"Okay." He nodded even though his body was still tense.

I understood how he felt. I wasn't thrilled with him going into a fight either, but this was our only chance at survival.

I connected with my wolf, calling her forward. It wasn't long before she was taking control. My vision became crisper as hair sprouted all over my body and my bones cracked. My clothes ripped off me, and soon I stood on four legs. When the shift was finally over, I surveyed the area and found Beth with light brown fur all over her body and Aidan with his black fur. Our wolves' fur was the same as our natural hair color. I'd always been curious what Beth's color was.

"You better stay close to me too." Finn appeared at my side and stared into my animal eyes. "You may be half-wolf, but you're the only family I have left. We need each other."

Those words softened me toward him, but now wasn't the time to be emotional. I howled, alerting the other wolves of my location.

I was glad Aidan and I couldn't mind link because I could tell he was pissed at what I'd done. But with their focus solely on me, it would be easier for the others to take them.

Just as I'd expected, the wolves perked up and glanced in my direction. They charged the grassy area where the majority of witches were.

The group split apart, six running left, six running right, and eight heading straight down the middle. They were circling us, intending to herd us into a group. What they didn't know was that we wanted to be together.

A wolf began running faster, and the witches turned their focus on it. They'd begun chanting when a scream came from the left, breaking whatever spell they had started.

I ran toward the noise and saw a wolf with its teeth in a female witch's arm. It thrashed its head as others nearby began casting a spell. Another wolf attacked the people focused on saving the girl.

That was their plan. Get our focus on saving our people and take us out one by one. We had to get off the defensive.

I growled as I ran at the wolf that was about to strike near us. I must have caught it off guard because I steamrolled him ten feet before he reacted.

Two wolves surrounded me as I realized my mistake. I'd put myself closer to the eight wolves with no one beside me.

I faced one of the other wolves as he attacked. His sharp teeth sank deep into my front right leg.

Pain radiated down my leg, and the longer I kept from defending myself, the worse the injury would be. The problem was, I had to determine how to get him off me without causing him to clamp down even harder.

Black fur flashed past me, and Aidan tore into the wolf. He bit down hard. The wolf loosened its hold on my leg. I spun away, limping.

Another wolf surged forward, and I stumbled to the ground, narrowly missing his attack.

Beth appeared beside me, snarling at the wolf.

Unfortunately, two others were also closing in.

"We need to help them." Coral's voice rang loudly from fifty feet away.

Three wolves took off after her to prevent her from getting close enough to help us.

I forced myself to ignore my injured leg; otherwise, I

would only get hurt worse. I pushed through the pain and faced the two wolves moving like one toward me. Aidan and Beth were embroiled in their fights. This was their chance to take me out.

If I didn't stay calm, I'd be dead within seconds. The two wolves split up to flank me. I would have to choose one to keep my eye on while the other attacked from behind. This was a lose-lose situation.

As I turned to glare at one, I heard the other spring its attack. I tried turning back around but stumbled with my hurt leg.

I expected to feel another jab of pain, but then wind blew past me, and I heard a loud thud and whimper as the wolf hit the ground.

"What did I say about staying close to me?" Finn's words could have passed for a growl if he had been a shifter. His eyes locked on the wolf getting back to its feet.

Finn had saved my life. The other wolf took the opportunity to charge. I waited until the last second, and then I dropped to the ground and rolled onto my back. The wolf lost its balance and fell on top of me. When its weight hit all four of my paws, I lifted with every ounce of strength I had to throw it. It only flew eight feet but hit the ground with a sickening crack on its side. I hoped I'd broken a rib, leg—hell, anything.

Aidan appeared right beside me, blood dripping down his face. He whimpered when he looked at my foreleg and then huffed and focused on the wolf trying to stand.

Not wasting his advantage, Aidan raced at him and sunk his teeth into its neck, digging in to hit the main artery. The wolf collapsed as blood poured from the wound.

I took in the chaos around us. Only a handful of wolves

were still alive, but several witches were lying still on the ground, covered in blood.

This wasn't supposed to happen.

Beth's sweet scent filled my nose, and her snout nudged me in the back.

I spun around and found blood on her. Shit. How hurt was she? I scanned her body and sighed in relief when I realized the blood wasn't hers.

"You won't kill any more of my family," Finn said, rage ringing in his voice. He pulled out a knife and charged the wolf.

The wolf hunkered down and charged. Finn lifted his free left hand and chanted some undistinguishable words, and the wolf fell back again. As soon as it hit the ground, he raised the knife high above his head and slammed it into the wolf's heart.

The wolf whimpered and thrashed until the overly sour scent of fear poured off him as it realized it was going to die. Finn kept his hands on the knife, digging it in deeper, his amber eyes burning into the wolf's fading vision.

I began trotting over to him, but Aidan stepped in front of me, shaking his head no.

The message was loud and clear. Finn could be out of his mind. There was so much anger in him. He could easily mistake me for an enemy wolf.

When the wolf took its last breath, Finn ripped the knife from its chest and faced me. "Let's go finish this." He headed back to the witches, who had the last wolf cornered.

"Take it to the cellar of my house, and chain it up. I'll be there shortly," Beatrice instructed two male witches. She turned toward me, and her eyes softened. "Let's get you inside and take care of that wound."

I nodded and limped to Beatrice's house. Aidan kept

pace beside me, and his eyes met mine.

This would have been an amazing time for a mind link. I was going to be okay. Hell, I'd be mostly healed by morning. That was a nice perk of having shifter genes.

Amethyst hurried to the front door and opened it for Aidan and me. "Beth, go change and come back here. Coral and Rowan will be here by the time you get back."

My nails clacked against the wood as I slowly climbed the stairs and went straight into our bedroom. The metallic smell of my blood and the pain were making me nauseous, but I powered through it. The best thing for me was to change back into human form and get the wound taken care of.

Aidan entered the room right after me and shut the door with his head.

We both called our wolves back. Our bones began to break again, and the fur disappeared from our bodies. I soon found myself on two legs, and we were both standing completely naked in front of each other.

My eyes took in every inch of his body. His abs were chiseled and his skin flawless. Warmth spread throughout my body as my gaze lowered. He was definitely not small.

He chuckled as he watched me. "You see something you like?"

"Nope, not at all." I would never admit that I was close to drooling. I walked over and kissed him. As I lifted my arm, I groaned and pulled away.

"Get dressed." He opened the closet and threw down a pair of jeans, some underwear, and a tank top. "We need to disinfect your wound."

"But I was enjoying..." I wanted to have at least a few minutes alone with him. I mean, he was naked, for Christ's sake.

"You can enjoy it later." A sexy-ass grin crossed his face. "You not getting an infection is a lot more important."

"Fine." He was right. We had other things to deal with. I took one last scan.

"Now." He arched an eyebrow, humor clear in his eyes.

Getting dressed went slower than I'd anticipated. I hadn't noticed how many movements caused the muscles in my arm to move. Ten minutes later, I was finally dressed, and that was with Aidan's help.

Downstairs, we found the same group from breakfast. Finn, Samuel, and Coral were sitting on the couch while the rest of the group was at the kitchen table.

As we passed them, it was hard not to notice the blood on Finn's face or the deep scratches on Samuel's arm.

We hadn't come out of this unscathed.

"Come here, dear." Beatrice stood from her chair and waved Sage to move down a few seats. "I've got some alcohol to clean your wound; then we'll put some healing herbs on it."

Not wanting to be rude, I hurried over. She picked up some cotton and soaked it with the disinfectant. I sat across from Sage, and Amethyst sat between her and Beth.

"Here, hold my hand." Aidan frowned as he held out his hand. "Squeeze it if it'll help."

Needing his touch, I took his hand and sucked in a deep breath as Beatrice placed the alcohol on my arm.

If I'd thought it hurt before, I'd been wrong. The alcohol made my arm feel like it was on fire. It was the section of my arm closest to my shoulder. He'd gone for my neck and missed.

Tears fell down my cheeks as she cleaned it.

I had to distract myself. "Has the wolf shifted back to his human form?"

"Yeah, he just has," Rowan said as she gave me a sad smile. "Someone used a spell to force him back to his human form. He refused to do it on his own."

"Figures. Men are scaredy cats." Beth nodded at me. "You know I'm right."

I tried to appear strong. "How many did we lose?" I tried to keep the emotion out of my voice, but my emotional and physical pain quivered through.

"We lost ten." Sage's eyes glistened with unshed tears. "The rest of the coven not with the wolf is preparing them for the death ritual."

"I'm so sorry." I felt responsible.

"It's not your fault, child." Beatrice shook her head. "They died protecting our destined leader. It was with honor."

It didn't make things better.

Beatrice picked up some green paste and applied it to my arm. "Let me bandage you up, and we'll all go down there and see what he has to say."

Within minutes, I was bandaged and ready to go. As I stood, the others followed suit.

"It's about damn time." Finn opened the front door.

Aidan frowned at my cousin. "She had wounds that needed to be cleaned and bandaged."

"I know. Otherwise, I'd have left without you all." Finn's voice was low in warning. "The next part will be the best."

His eagerness to get to the enemy wolf scared me. He enjoyed hurting wolf shifters. If this was any indication of what we might face once we got to the basement, there was no telling what to expect to happen in the next few short minutes.

CHAPTER TWENTY-TWO

Our group followed Beatrice and Amethyst outside and around the house. A stairwell beside the house led downstairs to a basement.

It looked like one of those staircases you'd see in a horror movie. The steps were concrete with no railing. The humidity was heavy, making it feel like I was breathing liquid instead of air.

Aidan's concerned eyes met mine. "You okay?"

Yeah, I wouldn't admit in front of everyone that I was spooked. I'd faced down twenty wolves without hesitation, but going down those damn stairs was giving me the willies. "I'm fine." I took his hand and tugged him next to me so we descended side by side.

The stairwell consisted of about twenty steps, and at the bottom, Beatrice opened the door to let the light from inside illuminate some of the darkness.

"Tell us who knows we're here," a loud, deep voice demanded.

A deep chuckle was the response.

Inside the basement, a witch stood in front of the naked

shifter, glaring at him. The shifter had his eyes to the ground with a smirk. He was purposely pissing off the witches.

Of course he'd be naked. He most likely hadn't brought clothes to change into after he shifted back.

We piled into the room, with Aidan on one side, Beth on the other, and Finn right behind me. Everyone else was behind us except for Amethyst and Beatrice, who made their way next to the male witch.

The ground was dirt, and the room was hot with moisture and no airflow. The sides were cement, but there were cobwebs woven throughout. There wasn't even a window down here.

Beatrice stared down the shifter. "Has he told you anything?"

"No, he hasn't." The vein in the witch's neck bulged. "He just chuckles after every damn question."

I had to piss the shifter off so he'd get reckless with his words. "That's unfortunate."

The shifter's head snapped up, and his eyes locked on me. "You're the girl, aren't you?"

"I'm not sure what you mean." I batted my eyelashes, smiling innocently at him.

His focus turned to Aidan and then Beth. "You are here. We were told we had a traitor who clung to her." He nodded at the place where my hand was wrapped in Aidan's.

"Traitor?" I arched an eyebrow, and Aidan's hand tensed. "I'm thinking you meant to say someone strong enough to see both sides of the story." He must not be from Aidan's pack since he didn't recognize the man.

"No, easily manipulated is more like it." The captive's breathing increased.

I tilted my head. "Well, you guys were obviously idiots to only bring twenty wolves against an entire coven."

Beth strolled over to stand beside me. "Must have had a death wish."

"Unless they didn't know." Aidan examined the shifter. "You must be from the Jones pack."

"If you think I'm impressed, you're quite mistaken." The guy sneered. "You're leaving me tied up here, surrounded by witches. You're worse than a traitor."

Wait... Jones... he was from Jacob's roommate's pack. I'd have to ask Jacob about it later because right now, this guy would enjoy the fact that I didn't know it. "What exactly have the witches done to you?"

"They cursed the original alpha." He wrinkled his nose in disgust and growled. "We had to split the original Murphy pack hundreds of years ago to keep an eye out for this abomination." He pointed at me, making the chains clang together.

"I mean your friends will be here any second to rescue you, right?" I figured if they were going to, they would've by now.

He winced.

"He's scared." Amethyst glanced at me. "And feels alone."

"So, no one is coming." Aidan smirked. "How does it feel to know you'll be dead in a matter of hours?"

"They may not know where you are, but they'll find you." He bared his teeth at Aidan. "Mark my words."

Beth's forehead crinkled with confusion. "Why wouldn't they tell them where we're located?"

"Because they were arrogant and didn't consider that we might be with witches who would protect us. They expected us to be alone and unprepared." Aidan leaned back on his heels and laughed humorlessly.

The guy's eyes darkened, confirming Aidan's theory.

"I guess there isn't much more to gather from him." We'd learned we hadn't been exposed—yet.

"Then let's go back upstairs," Coral said eagerly. "I hate being down here."

"I can't say I disagree." Samuel headed to the door and opened it.

I'd almost expected air to blow into the room, but with how deep the basement was, the room remained stagnant.

"I'll take care of him." Finn stepped between Beth and me and looked at Beatrice.

"I'm not sure—" she began, but he cut her off.

"Please, let me do this," Finn begged.

I'd never thought I'd hear someone actively hoping to kill another.

"I would appreciate it." The other male witch's shoulder sagged with relief. "I'm not sure I have it in me."

Beatrice sucked in a breath and glanced from Finn to the shifter. He was still staring at me with hatred. "Fine," she muttered.

The rest of us left Finn and the other male witch with the shifter.

Aidan

TONIGHT HAD BEEN WORSE than I could've ever imagined. Those wolves' sole purpose had been to kill Emma. I'd live with the horrible images of her fighting and getting injured for the rest of my life.

It worried me because Bradley hadn't been involved, which meant that another attack would be imminent. They would be waiting for their fighters to return to inform them whether Emma had been eliminated and other details before launching another fight. Both packs would be involved in the next battle. However, when the Jones pack wolves don't return by morning, it'll escalate their schedule.

But right now, I didn't want to burden Emma with that. She needed sleep to heal. I hated that she was now involved in a war.

She deserved happiness and freedom. Not to worry about a witch's curse. I loved her so damn much it hurt, and I'd do anything to never see her hurt like that again.

Emma

AIDAN and I headed upstairs to our room as the witches went to perform the ceremony for those who had died. I'd offered to go along with them, but they wanted Aidan and me to stay behind and get some rest. I was injured, and I still had so much to process. They said the ritual would start at midnight, so Aidan and I had this place to ourselves for the next thirty minutes.

As soon as we entered our bedroom upstairs, I pushed him into the wall.

Not missing a beat, his lips touched mine. They buzzed, and the taste of mint hit my senses. His tongue stroked my lips, asking for entrance into my mouth.

I opened my mouth, touching my tongue to his. The connection thrummed between us, and my wolf surged forward. A low growl came from my throat as I pushed him to the bed and climbed onto his lap. Even though my arm hurt, my need for him was stronger than ever. Fighting our connection had been stupid. We could have lost each other tonight.

Desperation crashed through me, and he grabbed my waist, digging his fingers into my sides. His hardness pressed against me, and I began rubbing, needing friction.

I bit his lower lip, and he groaned, pulling back a bit. "Dammit, Emma." He fisted his hands in my hair and smashed my lips against his. His hand slipped under my shirt and inched up my waist.

The musky scent of my arousal mixed with his, making me lightheaded. I wanted him so damn much.

He groaned. "We have to stop."

"No." My lips landed back on his, and he responded to my kiss again.

I went to tug his shirt over his head, but he caught my hand. "Are you sure you're ready?" He leaned back, and his eyes were glowing brightly, his wolf right at the front.

"Yes. It's stupid that we've waited this long."

"You deserve for it to be perfect." He pressed his lips to mine softly once more.

"This is perfect." I yanked on his shirt, angry that it was still a barrier between us. "I'm tired of waiting. I want you. Nothing will ever change that. You're it for me. I knew it four years ago, so please stop fighting this."

"Thank God. I don't want you hurting your arm any more than it already is. Let me take care of these." He removed his shirt, and his hands went to the bottom of mine, pulling it off slowly.

He threw our shirts on the ground as his lips went straight to my neck. He kissed me all the way down. He caressed my breast, but my black bra prevented him from touching my skin. I whimpered in protest.

"Patience." He chuckled as his lips went down my chest, and his hands slid around my back to unfasten my bra. He pulled away, slipping the straps over my shoulders.

His lips crashed against mine as his hand cupped my breast, and I ground against him, again enjoying the feeling of him teasing me.

He pulled his lips away and took my nipple into his mouth.

Heat flooded my body as his tongue made me feel things I'd never experienced before. "God, please." I needed him. My wolf surged forward. She'd been wanting this for way too long, and she was desperate for the bond to be completed.

I stood and slowly removed my pants and panties. Aidan did the same. He was gorgeous sitting there on the bed, waiting for me.

My eyes devoured all of him, and soon, I was sliding back onto his lap.

His fingers dug into my waist as he slid us to the headboard of the bed. He stared straight into my eyes. "I love you. But let's take it slow. I don't want to hurt you."

"I love you too." As the words had left my lips, I guided him inside me.

And as he filled me, emotions collided inside my heart and my mind. I began moving as his lips lowered to my neck once more. His teeth grazed my skin, and I whimpered with need. I wanted him to claim me.

That must have been what he'd needed because he bit into me, merging his wolf with mine.

When he pulled away, I didn't break the rhythm of our

connection and placed my lips on his neck. Unlike him, I bit into his neck immediately, and blood filled my mouth.

Holy shit. His words filled my head. *You are amazing.*

I'm so glad you're mine now. I increased our pace, and he followed my lead.

In minutes, our emotions tangled, and we were both about to climax. I claimed his lips once more and linked to him. *I love you.*

Our bodies shook together as our bond completed.

I love you too, he whispered in my mind.

Once we'd stilled, something clicked into place between us, solidifying everything. The dark void inside me began to pulse. It pulsed so hard it felt like the house was shaking.

"Earthquake," Aidan said as he rolled me off him and onto the bed.

The walls shook, and glass broke somewhere downstairs. I jumped to my feet, grabbed my clothes from the ground, and slowly dressed as I tried to keep my balance.

"We need to get outside," Aidan shouted. He threw his clothes on and helped me get dressed quicker. "The upstairs could collapse."

We ran out of the room and to the stairs. I wasn't sure how it was possible, but the ground began shaking even harder.

I scanned the living room as we rushed to the door. It shocked me that even though the ground was jarring violently, nothing had broken except for a vase, which had fallen off a table. It was as if the house was protected from falling apart.

We made it outside, and Beatrice and Amethyst met us in the yard.

They both focused on me, and then the ground began to still.

"What the hell was that?" Aidan shook his head as he surveyed the surrounding area. "Earthquakes aren't even common here."

"She caused it." Beatrice pointed to me. "Her magic has been awakened."

"What?" The cold void in me was now warm, but it still felt trapped somehow.

Her eyes landed on me. "Do you feel different?"

"Well, yeah. But it's still like my magic is enchained." It was odd, but I instinctively knew that.

"It's because it's time for you to find the others." Beatrice touched my shoulder. "You've awakened all of your magic. The earthquake was felt across the country, and now the other girls will have a mark too."

"Wait. What?" None of this was making sense. "I thought I was the only one."

"No, there is more than one. A star has five points and can't be alone. You were the key to unlocking the prophecy." She glanced at Amethyst and grinned. "Now you must find the other women like you and create the council that will lead over all."

"Okay." All of my doubts were gone. I immediately knew that the void had been my witch magic. Now I had to follow this through. The Hallowed Guild needed to be stopped, and I would be the one to do it.

The End

ABOUT THE AUTHOR

Jen L. Grey is a *USA Today* Bestselling Author who writes Paranormal Romance, Urban Fantasy, and Fantasy genres.

Jen lives in Tennessee with her husband, two daughters, and two miniature Australian Shepherd. Before she began writing, she was an avid reader and enjoyed being involved in the indie community. Her love for books eventually led her to writing. For more information, please visit her website and sign up for her newsletter.

Check out my future projects and book signing events at my website.
www.jenlgrey.com

ALSO BY JEN L. GREY

The Marked Wolf Trilogy

Moon Kissed

Chosen Wolf

Broken Curse

Wolf Moon Academy Trilogy

Shadow Mate

Blood Legacy

Rising Fate

The Royal Heir Trilogy

Wolves' Queen

Wolf Unleashed

Wolf's Claim

Bloodshed Academy Trilogy

Year One

Year Two

Year Three

The Half-Breed Prison Duology (Same World As Bloodshed Academy)

Hunted

Cursed

The Artifact Reaper Series

Reaper: The Beginning

Reaper of Earth

Reaper of Wings

Reaper of Flames

Reaper of Water

Stones of Amaria (Shared World)

Kingdom of Storms

Kingdom of Shadows

Kingdom of Ruins

Kingdom of Fire

The Pearson Prophecy

Dawning Ascent

Enlightened Ascent

Reigning Ascent

Stand Alones

Death's Angel

Rising Alpha

Printed in Great Britain
by Amazon